OBJECTS IN MIRROR
ARE CLOSER THAN THEY APPEAR

OBJECTS IN MIRROR
ARE CLOSER THAN THEY APPEAR

Selected Short Stories

by

Max Layton

Mosaic Press
Oakville-New York-London

Canadian Cataloguing in Publication Data

Layton, Max, 1946-
    Objects in the Mirror...

ISBN 0-88962-541-7
I. Title.

PS8573.A89025 1993   C813'.54   C93-093408-3
PR9199.3.L389025 1993

Published by MOSAIC PRESS, P.O. Box 1032 Oakville, Ontario, L6J 5E9, Canada.   Offices and warehouse at 1252 Speers Road, Units #1&2, Oakville, Ontario, L6L 5N9, Canada.

Mosaic Press acknowledges the assistance of the Canada Council and the Ontario Arts Council in support of its publishing programme.

Copyright © Max Layton, 1993
Design by Patty Gallinger
Typeset by Jackie Ernst
Printed and Bound in Canada.

ISBN 0-88962-541-7 PB

Cover Art by Jan Winton
Title: The Audition, 1986, Serigraphy

MOSAIC PRESS:

In Canada:
        MOSAIC PRESS, 1252 Speers Road, Units 1&2, Oakville, Ontario, L6L 5N9, Canada. P.O. Box 1032, Oakville, Ontario L6J 5E9

In the U.K.:
        John Calder (Publishers) Ltd., 9-15 Neal Street, London, WCZH 9TU, England.

For My Mother, Boschka,
1922-1984

ACKNOWLEDGEMENT

"The Myth of Joel Ickerman, "Mandi", and *"In The Middle of Things"* appeared in **Descant**.

"My Yarmulka" appeared in **The Antigonish Review.**

"When John Godfrey Came to" appeared in **Exile.**

Table of Contents

IN THE MIDDLE OF THINGS

I am living in the basement of a small apartment building where I work as the janitor. My marriage has broken up and I am having trouble getting out of bed. Some tuneless modern music is playing on the FM and I am too lethargic to change it. My legs are thin and my skin is white and I notice this on Fridays when there is a seminar I have to give to first year students in philosophy. (I am a third year student myself and am supposedly attending classes although lately I haven't had the strength.) I stumble to the bathroom, wash and shave. I take some satisfaction in seeing what progress the lines on my face have made as I scrape away the beard.

For a few hours I am myself again and I terrify my students by proving St. Anselm's argument for the existence of God. One of the kids is a Jewish atheist and fights me desperately. I refute his counterarguments one by one. By the end of the seminar he is trembling and his cheeks are red and sweating.

"Nobody said philosophy was a game," I remind him. "It can demolish the foundations of all your thinking."

"Then...then God exists?"

"Let's just say," I answer, looking at the clock, "that He exists for the moment. We'll see if He still exists by the time we get to Nietzsche. Class dismissed."

In the hall he runs after me. "I've got it!" he says. "Just because we think God exists, it doesn't follow that He does."

"Good for you," I reply. "It was hundreds of years before Kant came to the same conclusion."

"You mean, I'm right?"

1

He is already preening himself. I realise that if I don't take him down a peg he'll be insufferable for the rest of the year.

"Unfortunately, by your own reasoning," I say, "it doesn't follow from thinking you're right, that you are."

I have done my duty. Either he will sign up for philosophy again in the fall or he will do something sensible like study mechanical engineering.

Outside, the air is cold and I am short of breath. Passing someone on the crowded street, I have an insane desire to plunge a knife into his chest. My fists are knotted and a little further on I slam into someone's shoulder and send him spilling to the ice.

"Watch where you're going!" he shouts.

He is an old man with a florid face and ridiculously long legs.

"I'm sorry," I say, and help him to his feet.

Back in my room I have a coughing fit and then I pull out my guitar and write half a song. Then I read the newspaper and eat two boiled eggs. The room is dark, even with the lights on. In the fall I stapled sheets of plastic over the windows to keep out the wind. Then the snow came and buried me in.

I lie back on the bed. My beard is growing and my teeth are slowly turning yellow. My tongue has discovered a cavity and keeps poking into it.

My landlady is on the phone. It is four in the morning and, as usual, she is unable to sleep. Her name is Madame Lajoie. She is sixty years old and reads too many newspapers. She reads about violence in the streets, about gangs of perverted youths who have nothing better to do than to rape defenseless widows - especially sixty-year-old widows with worried innocent eyes.

"Don't worry, Madame, I will look after you."

"You! You don't heeven keep clean the halls."

"Madame," I lie. "I cleaned them last week the halls."

"The girls in number ten are not paying the rent, they tell me the place is so dirty."

"Madame, the girls in number ten are lesbians. *Lesbiennes,* I say in French, hoping there is such a word and that she knows what it means. I hear her gasp at the other end.

"*Monseigneur!*" she says. "Don't tell me that."

"But it's true, Madame, *c'est vrai.* They hate young men like me. They want to get rid of me. Take a dangerous journey downtown and see for yourself if you don't believe me."

2

"Michael, I am alone in this world. My husband is dead. Please understand. I must have those rents."

"Don't worry, Madame. I will rent the empty apartments. I will clean everything..."

It is snowing and the snow is melting on my head. I have trudged halfway up the mountain to the white highrise where my baby daughter lives with my wife. I have decided to surrender after all.

The song I still have not finished is entitled: *If It Hurts So Bad It Must Be Love.*

I speak into the intercom. There is a hesitation before she presses the buzzer which lets me in. In the elevator, the snow falling from my hair gets into my eyes. I open my coat and my body, heated by its recent climb, gives off a strong, stale odour.

"Hold me," I whisper when she opens her door.

"Mike, are you all right?"

"I don't know," I say. "I feel like I'm falling apart."

She lets me hold her in the hallway for a long time and then we step inside. We make love almost immediately.

Afterwards, I remember, I made us hot milk and honey and we sat facing each other on the bed. She too had enjoyed the love-making, she said. And I remember thinking how beautiful she was - now that I had conquered her again. It was as if someone has smeared my eyes with vaseline. Her eyes were shining and I no longer saw the stretch marks on her skin.

I stayed a week.

And then we were standing in a field below her building. Spring had come suddenly and we had to be careful where we walked because the earth was wet. I was going to classes again and for one of them, Natural Science, I had to do an experiment: *Using a fixed point of reference, e.g., a chimney, map the positions of five bright stars. Four hours later, map again. Measure the difference.*

"Janice," I said. "They've moved sixty degrees. Do you know what that means?"

No answer. She was standing with her arms folded, her head tilted at the starlit sky.

"Look," I said. "It's the most beautiful thing. Four hours is one sixth of a day, right?"

No answer.

"Well, the entire night sky has rotated exactly one sixth of 360 degrees. Janice, I've proved that the earth is round."

"I think the stars are beautiful just as they are."

"Of course they are. Of course they are, damn it, but--"

"I think part of their beauty is their mystery."

"I agree. But surely part of their beauty is also the fact that they're governed by laws. And even more beautiful--"

Here Janice turned away and began climbing the path back up to her building.

"--even more mysterious, is the fact that we can understand them."

"You understand them. I'm going in."

"Okay, go!" I shouted. And then I ran after her, talking smoothly, saying, "Honey, what's the matter? What's the problem?"

"I'm not one of your students, Mike. I have ideas of my own."

"Of course you do, Honey. Who said you didn't?"

Her face pinched and she tried to run. I caught her by the back of her sweater and pulled her towards me. "Are you crazy?" I said. "I just wanted to--"

She whirled on me. "Leave me alone!"

I let her go and her foot slipped and then she was up again and I knew it was over.

She slowed half way up the hill, at the point where a thicket overgrew the path. Her torso was lost in the darkness and all I could see, as it rose disembodied above me, was the lunar indifference of her child-widened ass.

"I just wanted to share it with you!" I shouted. And then I made my way across the muddy field.

———————

I have taken the plastic off my windows and opened the door to the yard at the back. It is filled with old mattresses, bits of wood, broken bits of glass. In a corner, under a shack used for storing screens and double windows, a yellow threadbare cat has given birth to kittens. I put some milk out for them. They are lousy with fleas.

I have rented all the apartments and one of the new tenants, Dennis, is becoming a friend. He is tall, blond. His hair is thinning. He has a large, manly chin and the hurt-looking eyes of a small boy. His mother died when he was seven. He has been writing a revolutionary new novel for several years and in the meantime lives off a stipend his father gives him once a month.

The one time Dennis took me with him, his father sat in a straight-backed chair and stroked the neck of his Labrador Retriever. The meeting between father and son was cold and formal and lasted all of five minutes.

"Well, that's the old man," Dennis said when we left. He sounded bitter although his father had given him a cheque.

"How come he never remarried?" I asked.

Dennis shrugged. "Ever read Konrad Lorenz?"

I said that I had.

"Then you know his theory of redirected aggression."

"That's when a dog snaps at the air instead of another dog's throat, isn't it?"

"Exactly. Well, if Lorenz had studied my father's devotion to pets, he would have realised there is also such a thing as redirected affection." His small, hurt eyes looked at me, looked away again. "I don't think he even misses my mother."

We were on a main street by then, walking side by side along the sidewalk. It was drizzling and a rather homely girl with rat-coloured hair squeezed past us and hurried on.

"How'd you like to get into that!" Dennis grinned, giving me a nudge. I gathered he was uncomfortable and wished to change the subject.

"Not my type," I obliged.

"No? Fussy, eh? What's your type?"

"I seem to go for the two extremes. Either cold Nordic goddesses or black-haired passionate Delilahs. I can't stand in-betweens."

"Good," he said. "That leaves all the more for me."

We laughed and for some strange reason, quite spontaneously, started running very fast.

———

We are obsessed by sex and women - in that order. It is incredible to us that every one of them *has* one of them. They are truly superior beings. How can they take it so calmly? We watch them walking with it nonchalantly, sitting on it, sometimes squeezing it when they cross their legs. It is amazing that they don't fall frothing to the floor, their bodies writhing in ecstacy.

"I don't think they can actually feel it," Dennis confides over a drink.

We are like two wild African dogs hunting a particularly skittish herd. We spend hours in night clubs eyeing them, sizing them up, circling them ever so warily, careful lest we break our cover - which is that we just happened to drop in and couldn't care less about what we know they're sitting on, in the darkness, underneath the table.

In the morning, Dennis drops into my armchair with an exhausted self-satisfied grin. His shirt is half open and I can see that his neck is covered with hickeys.

"We fucked for hours," he says. "She had to beg me to stop." His head lolls and for a minute I think he is asleep. Then he opens his eyes and confesses to the almighty ceiling: "What can I say? I just can't get enough!"

My own obsession is somewhat different. I also can't get enough and yet, sometimes, right in the middle of things, I am filled with revulsion. Take, for example, the bank teller I pick up every Wednesday at exactly five o'clock. I escort her to my room and we quickly get undressed. She is French-Canadian, with a body so perfect - and yet so small - that, instead of an hour-glass figure, she looks more like an egg-timer.

She also has buck teeth and large brown eyes and reminds me of a chipmunk. I tell her to lie on her stomach. A mistake! There, in the middle of her back, is a small, black mole. I lose my erection at the sight of it. She looks questioningly at me over her shoulder. Her face is radiant with obedience and love. She swivels and takes me in her mouth. She cries when I tell her to give up. She says she has never done that for a man before, not even when they begged...

Or take Arlene, my old high school sweetheart, who looks at me shrewdly and says that what I want is revenge...

Or Georgina, who once said that my poems were contradictory. *Contradictory?!*

This was not the response I expected. I expected awe, sympathy, curiosity. At the very least, I expected her to keep getting undressed. But she was absorbed in my manuscript.

"Look at this," she went on relentlessly, flipping the pages and spilling them across my bed. "Here you say that if a woman is ripe enough, it's a man's duty to pluck her - never mind how she feels about it. But five poems later you're upset because all some woman wanted you for was a fuck. You cry blue murder because your wife has left and then, in another poem, you claim that marriage is a trap to steal a man's freedom." (Here she propped some pillows against my headrest and leaned back with her hands behind her neck.) "You know what I think? I think you don't like women..."

Or Clarissa, who suddenly took her clothes off and walked pigeon-toed towards me while I tried to tell her that I didn't love her and she said she felt the same way...

Or that extraordinary afternoon when I had three different women in a row, which I mention not in a bragging way but to indicate that something was wrong. Because, if I was the seducer, why, when the day was over, did I feel so used? Because, let me tell you Georgina - you untroubled, unsympathetic bitch - I am astonished at how passive a man is in all this. I am astonished at how superfluous I suddenly discovered I was when my wife left and it turned out she was the one with the kid.

"What are you thinking about?" Dennis is saying.

"Nothing."

"Nothing, eh? Maybe that's why you look like somebody just kneed you in the *cojones.*"

He lights a cigarette and, crossing his legs, squints sceptically at me through the smoke.

"I'm thinking," I reply, "that women have a tremendous advantage over us. They know very, very precisely who they are."

"And you don't?"

"I know what I want to do. I know what I want to achieve. But a woman...women don't stake their whole lives on becoming astronomers or philosophers or mechanical engineers. They just are. Do you see what I'm driving at? They have no illusions."

"*Vive la différence*, that's all."

I snort derisively and Dennis goes on:

"I think you're talking abstractions. If you ask me, the main advantage women have is that they can fuck just about anyone they want, when they want."

"They can also *not* fuck when they don't want."

"So?"

"So haven't you noticed, Dennis? Haven't you noticed how very little you and I matter in any of this?"

I am also learning how to hypnotise. I have read several books about it and have memorized a formula. Dennis is eager to be my first subject. He believes it will help him overcome the writer's block which has been preventing him from getting down to his novel. He tells me again that its theme will be the divided self - the split between the rational and the creative sides of the brain.

"If you're right-handed like I am," he says, "the left side of your brain controls the right side of your body. The left side of the brain is dominant, verbal, rational. But the right side is still a mystery. It seems to be the source of our creativity. I think the great mystics tapped into it and called it soul. And I think, under hypnosis, maybe..."

He shrugs his shoulders reverently, as if to suggest that the possibilities are inexhaustible.

"I can't promise anything," I say.

He stubs out his cigarette. I turn off all the lights except the one in the kitchen. "What do I do?" he asks.

I tell him to lie back on the bed. His face is grey in the pale, refracted light. I tell him to breathe deeply and relax. I say the same words over and over. His mouth falls open. I order his right arm to rise against his will. The muscles in his neck contract. His right arm twitches on the bed beside him and then slowly, jerkily, lifts into the air. I am saying:

"Your arm will remain in the air until I tell you to put it down. No matter how hard you try, you cannot put it down. It is your right arm. You cannot put it down. You have surrendered control. The left side of your brain has surrendered control. You are now thinking with the right side of your brain. You are thinking with the right side only. You are thinking with the creative side of your soul and you are going to tell me what you are thinking...now."

I never did find out, although I hypnotised him many times that summer. He smiled. His arm fluttered. He made sounds, but they were unintelligible to me although they seemed soft and happy, like a baby cooing to itself.

"You will wake up," I said, "when I tell you to lower your arm. When you wake up, you will not remember anything I have said. Lower your arm."

He yawned, stretched. And then he sat up with a start. "What happened?" he asked.

"Don't you remember?"

"No," he said. "Nothing. Did we contact the right hemisphere?"

"I think so," I said.

"Well, shit, man! Don't keep me in suspense. What did I say?"

"Nothing. Nothing I could understand, Dennis. I'm sorry. It was like listening to a very happy baby. You know how a baby coos sometimes?"

He nodded his head.

"Well, it was like that."

He was quiet and I could see that he was disappointed.

"We could try again," I suggested. "It was really quite beautiful. Something very special."

Classes have started. It is September and I am in fourth year and on Fridays I delight in terrifying the students in my seminar by hypnotising them. Usually I take them on imaginary vacations to Eden-like islands but sometimes, when a brave one volunteers, I conduct experiments. I am fascinated by memory, by how a person can be made to forget anything - even one's own name - and by the intensity with which a memory can be relived. One girl, for instance, said she could feel the water in her mother's womb and another frightened me, by hysterically screaming that she was bleeding, when I took her back to the age of eleven.

I see Dennis less and less. He has a steady girlfriend. Her name is Sylvia and I don't know what he likes about her. She is larger than he is, with a moon-shaped face and freckled, sun-allergic skin. She shakes my hand when I meet her and looks at me with a cold and quizzical eye. She has a trick of lifting her left eyebrow as if to take your measure and this, I conclude at the end of the evening, is the only expression she is capable of.

"She's got an honours degree in psych," Dennis tells me next morning. "Graduated top in her class."

"She seems intelligent..."

"But you think she's uptight, right?"

"Well, I..."

"Never mind," he says. "To tell you the truth, she scares the hell out of me. She's so far ahead of me intellectually it isn't even funny. But emotionally, emotionally it's like she's a little girl inside. It's like I'm giving birth, Mike. Sometimes, when we make love, when I get her to the point where she starts moving - I don't know how to express it - it makes me feel worthy."

But I noticed, as the weeks wore on, that his face took on a harried look and that his eyes, when I met him occasionally in the street, refused to meet mine. "How's it going?" I'd say and he'd laugh and tell me too vehemently about progress on his novel. And once, when I saw him through the window of a restaurant, he was sitting alone with his shoulders stooped, staring blankly.

The good weather ended and the leaves fell. I put plastic on my windows and closed the door on the kittens which had grown up and gone.

And then Sylvia phoned.

She swept into my room wearing a long leather coat which she unbuttoned but did not remove. I made her a cup of coffee and she sat down.

"It's Dennis," she said. "I suppose you know that I left him?"

"No," I said. "I didn't. I haven't talked to him in ages."

"He's been acting peculiar. He keeps calling me late at night, writing me letters."

An eyebrow lifted on the surface of the moon. The moon smiled. Evidently, I was owed some sort of explanation.

"In the end it just got ridiculous. He kept calling me 'his woman'. Can you imagine? 'You must be out of your mind,' I said. 'This is the twentieth century. I'm willing to be your friend, your lover. But I'm nobody's woman.' It got to the point where he was trying to make me say it on my knees. 'Say it anyway,' he said. 'Say I'm your man and you're my woman.'"

"And did you?"

"I left."

The moon rose and fumbled with its buttons.

"He needs a friend, Mike. That's the only reason I came."

———

I recognize the symptoms immediately: the stale odour, the rumpled bathrobe, the rumpled hair. He is listless, unshaven. His bed is unmade. There are dirty clothes in a corner. An ashtray has been knocked over and its contents lie on the floor.

I open a window and he shivers a little. He pulls his bathrobe around him more tightly and sits down on the bed.

"Sylvia and I had an argument," he says. "We split up."

"I know. She asked me to drop in."

His eyes narrow and skitter around the room. "That's very considerate of her." His voice is tentative, probing. He lights a cigarette and squints at me through the smoke. "What did she tell you?"

"Nothing much. Just that you'd split up. She thought you could use a friend."

His face flushes. He is grateful, he says.

"She's some woman, Mike. But too egg-head for me. I couldn't get her to admit her feelings."

"I never thought she was your type."

He nods and lies back on the bed. I tell him to close his eyes.

"I wish I'd never met her," he says.

"I know how you feel," I say. He lies quietly while I speak the words he needs and then his right arm lifts into the air.

I take him back to his childhood, to a summer when his family rented a cottage beside the ocean at Cape Cod. I send him splashing into the combers of his favorite memory and he comes running, giggling, his skinny white legs scampering back up the beach to where his mother is still sitting beside his father and he shows them the water he has captured so cunningly in his tiny plastic pail.

When he lowers his arm, I say, it will be exactly as if his relationship with Sylvia had never been.

THE TOUCH

He had inherited his grandmother's eyebrows. He was only twenty years old but already they bristled and angled sharply upward. They gave his face a menacing look. That, and the fact that he was tall and solidly built. In high school they had been after him to play football. But it turned out that the coach merely wanted him to anchor the line and Mike wasn't much of a joiner anyway.

He plunged his mop into the bucket and spread its wet grey strands across the green linoleum of the stairs. He felt guilty because he hadn't washed them the week before nor, for that matter, the week before that. He was amazed none of the tenants in the building had complained. Not that it would have done them any good - the landlady was terrified of him - but all the same it was amazing what people would put up with.

Nor was Mike really a janitor. The job just paid the rent while he went to school. He had had an argument with his father some time before and eventually had been asked to leave home. It was only then that he had discovered he couldn't get a student loan because his father was too wealthy. The absurd injustice of this rankled as he washed each green linoleum tile.

In the bucket, here and there, a few islands of rainbow-coloured soap still floated on the water's greasy surface. He wrung out the mop and watched the dirty water run through the fingers of his left hand. The mop was old and in some of the corners had left soft pieces of rope huddled like obsequious mice.

Outside it was late afternoon and the sunlight hurt his eyes. The local toughs were sitting on a nearby verandah drinking beer. They watched him as he ducked through the small door that led to his apartment in the basement. It was a cramped little place, but in the summer, in its dark proximity to the earth, it was moist and cool.

He began to undress. He needed a bath. But a kind of listlessness stole over him and he sank back on his bed and looked around the room. A pile of dirty sheets lay heaped in a corner. Ashtrays overflowed. There were plates on the floor. A fine dust had settled over everything: the radiators, the overhead pipes, the hundreds of books and magazines which, sideways, open, straight up and down, occupied the chairs and tables of the room. To his immediate right and just above his head, resting on a ledge, was C.I. Lewis' *Mind and the World Order* - still open, its back broken at page 176, the exact point at which Mike had stopped reading - not just it, but anything, more than a month before.

He looked at it and began to laugh. He remembered how his professor had told him, in all seriousness, that there was no reason why man could not be omniscient. Mike had watched while, as he spoke, the professor had opened two packets of sugar and poured their contents into the ashtray. Then, carefully stirring his coffee, the professor had lifted his cup to his lips and promptly gagged on the first swallow.

The laugh made him feel good. Gave him new energy. The mood carried him into the kitchen, for once with some dishes in his hands. He made himself a cup of coffee and a couple of boiled eggs. He ate them listening to the radio and afterwards smoked a cigarette.

He had been walking for some time along narrow streets with screaming kids and old men with pipes in their mouths. The sun was setting in the window of a Catholic church. He watched it flare there for a while, staining its stained-glass Christ, until it seemed to Mike that he too was an onlooker at that ancient sacrifice. Overhead, the streetlamps began buzzing and then came on. A chill ran through Mike's body. He turned and walked as quickly as he could until he reached the main street and was slowed by the jostling crowd.

A number of people had stopped and were watching something on the other side. A naked women was dancing in the second-storey window of a discotheque. The lighting was arranged in such a way that only her shadow could be seen against the window pane. As she dipped and swivelled to a beat no one in the street could hear, Mike watched the crowd watching her.

A panhandler was working the crowd intently, methodically, not at all with the boozy indifference or the angry contempt of most panhandlers he'd seen. He noticed Mike staring at him and quickly gave him a wink. "Nice, eh?" he said, jerking his head toward the girl in the window.

Mike nodded and, a little embarrassed, looked across the street. The first girl had been replaced by another. This one taller with longer hair. He watched as she caressed the twin umbrella's of her breasts and rode a teasing shaft between her thighs. But, although he was careful not to show it, he kept his eye on the panhandler, intrigued by the evident success of his technique.

He was a little fellow, shorter than most of the women who gave him money. There was something wrong with his left leg and he skillfully exploited this for sympathy by nevertheless taking rapid steps, as if his whole body were saying, "See, I'm doing my best. Look how hard I try." Mike noticed that he always approached a couple from the woman's side, his hand gesticulating earnestly, his boyish black hair falling greasily over his sensitive, intelligent face.

"Looks like you're doing pretty good," Mike said in as folksy a manner as he could muster. The panhandler shot Mike a look of scrutiny and then, quite suddenly, broke out in a broad smile and came closer, proffering his hand. It was smooth and wiry, and practically disappeared in Mike's large grasp.

"The name's Jim," the panhandler said. "What's yours?"

Mike told him but the little fellow had already darted away after another likely-looking prospect. When he came back he sidled up to Mike and, with the air of a magician not wanting to give his best trick away, showed him the edge of a dollar bill before he plunged it into the recesses of his ill-fitting clothes. Carefully chosen clothes though, Mike imagined, noticing how the panhandler's earnest image was matched by vest and tie. Intrigued more than ever, Mike decided that the best way to find out about the fellow was to play up to his obvious vanity.

"Don't they ever say no?" Mike asked, deliberately stressing 'they' and thus implying 'us'.

Again the appraising look. Suspicion followed by a grin.

"Not if I choose them right," the panhandler said. "I've been doing this so many years I can pick 'em in my sleep...You wouldn't happen to have a cigarette on you, would you?"

Mike dutifully fetched the pack out of his pocket and held it open. The panhandler helped himself.

"I knew you did," the panhandler said with a grin. "I seen the bulge." The two of them lit up from Mike's silver lighter. The panhandler held its flame in the curl of his tiny hand, sucking the smoke against his teeth and inhaling deeply. "Yeah, I'm the best there is," he said, gesturing eloquently with his cigarette.

"I'll bet you are!" Mike chimed in, inwardly amazed at the fellow's naive conceit while at the same time almost subliminal images came to him of boxcars swaying in the night, men looking out at the countryside through the rain, Saskatchewan wheat, the smell of the ocean at Vancouver.

Again the quick look of scrutiny and then the disarming smile. "You know," the panhandler said, "I can get what I want out of just about anybody. But every once in a while it feels good to pay my own way. How about I buy you a beer?"

It was Mike's turn to be wary. He sensed he might be falling for a con but he couldn't imagine what it was. There was nothing he was afraid to lose and, besides, the thought of out-panhandling a panhandler was too good to resist.

"Sure," Mike said and followed as the panhandler turned abruptly and led the way down the street.

The restaurant was crowded and hot and filled with smoke. A jukebox was playing so loudly in the corner that people had to shout even louder to make themselves heard. Mike noticed that they kept bobbing up and down at their tables, hugging each other or switching places to get away. The room smelled of old coats and stale perfume.

"Two quarts and a plate of fries," the panhandler said to the waiter who, a minute later, could be heard shouting the same thing to the cook behind the counter. A sixty-year-old woman with dyed blond hair suddenly stood to her feet and with her arms outstretched, her whole body swaying, began singing a song from the Second World War. Soon half the room had joined in and a guy came from several tables away and began cuddling her and kissing her neck until she sank beneath the weight of his affection into her chair. He was still clinging to her when, over her shoulder, he saw the panhandler for the first time. He stopped kissing the woman and came over. Like everyone else, he had obviously been drinking and leaned for support against the back of a chair.

"How you doing?" he said. He had leaned forward and was smiling expansively. Mike noticed that he was wearing several large rings on the fingers of both hands.

"Not bad," the panhandler replied. He shifted uneasily in his chair, making it plain that he did not want to continue the conversation.

"Who's your friend?"

"Somebody you don't know," the panhandler said.

The other fellow reared back and allowed himself to laugh a little too loudly and a little too long.

"Has your Mr. X got a cigarette he can spare?"

Mike, who had already begun to feel uncomfortable without knowing why, quickly offered him one. The fellow picked up Mike's lighter and gave himself a light, puffing a few times to make certain it was burning evenly.

"Thanks," he said, studying the lighter as if debating whether to walk away with it. Then he dropped it back on the table and sauntered off.

The gesture was insulting and Mike felt the muscles on his chest tightening like hoops around a barrel. At the same time, he didn't want to interfere in the panhandler's private world.

"Who was that?" Mike asked.

"An asshole," the panhandler snapped. "He thinks he runs this place and everybody in it." The panhandler would have said more but just then the waiter rushed over and served the beer and fries. The panhandler made a show of reaching deep into his pockets and pulling out several crumpled dollar bills. "Keep the change," he said.

Mike remembered how, intense, skipping on his gimpy leg, the panhandler had hustled all the way to the restaurant.

"I stay away from men with ties," he had said. "When a man's wearing a tie he's tight, you know? I mean, he's out to prove something. Everybody's like that. Everybody thinks they're the best, you know what I mean? But a guy with an open shirt now. Maybe he's on vacation. For sure he's taking it easy. He doesn't mind sharing his wealth, you know? It stands to reason."

The panhandler's pitch, when Mike overheard it, was simple, straight-forward and irresistible:

"Listen," he said to a man with a droopy moustache and a tailored jean jacket, "I'm desperate. I got to have a drink. I'm an alcoholic. I can't help myself. Give me a break. I know I can be honest with you. Fifty cents, that's all I need..."

It worked every time.

Mike took a swallow of his beer and reached for a french fry. It was cold to the touch and when he put it in his mouth it tasted like paste. He wanted to spit it out but the table didn't have any napkins. Neither did the tables nearby. However, each did have a plate of fries that no one was touching.

"You see," the panhandler explained, "this is supposed to be a restaurant. They're not allowed to serve liquor without food."

The jukebox started up again and several couples began to dance. They clung to each other fiercely. There was hardly enough room for them between the tables and chairs. Mike wanted to ask the panhandler about so many things, the places he'd been, the people he'd met, about living on the bum. Surely the panhandler had seen so much. But the jukebox played too loud and the panhandler was already finishing his beer. It seemed to Mike that the little fellow had been acting distant and nervous for quite a while, since the guy with the rings had come over, in fact. Somehow Mike was no longer part of the panhandler's 'inner circle', no longer one of those to whom the secret of the touch could be revealed.

The panhandler pushed back his chair. "Got to take a leak," he announced and hurried off to the john. Mike watched his thin back disappear into the throng on the other side of the room. He looked at the faces around him. They were old, their eyes glistening, their mouths wet and wide open, as if wanting to suck a few laughs out of each others' throats while there was still time.

Out of the corner of his eye he caught sight of the panhandler making his way back through the crowd. But he was walking more slowly than usual, with his head bowed, and when he sat down Mike could see that there were tears in his eyes.

"What happened?" Mike said, his heart going out to the little runt, wanting to comfort him and yet not knowing what to do.

A long moment passed. The panhandler sat there silently striking the table with the side of his left hand. "That bastard!" he finally said. "That goddam bastard. He thinks he runs this whole place."

"Who?" Mike said. "You mean the guy with the rings? What did he do?"

"What did he do!" the panhandler sneered. "Why, he just shoved me up against the wall and punched me in the stomach, that's all. He just said that if he ever caught me in here again he'd beat my brains in. It's nothing to get upset about!" The anger left him. He slumped back in his chair and let the air sigh out of his lungs in a long, low whistle. "You see, this place is important to me," he went on matter-of-factly after a while. "Every bum has to have some place where the waiters know him, where he can count on a drink if he's been sick or busted or something's happened so he hasn't had a chance to hustle. Besides, I got friends here, good friends. I can't let this guy squeeze me out."

"Well, he's not going to do it while I'm around," Mike said. "Go punch him in the nose right now. I'll back you up."

The panhandler shook his head. "You don't understand," he said. "If him and me cause any trouble, the waiters'll just kick the both of us out. I can't afford to get in a fight with him, even if I win. And the thing is, he's waiting for me at the front door. He's gonna come after me when I go outside, I just know it."

Mike was more than touched. He was outraged. At the same time, he felt a kind of release, a God-like elation, a profound moral yearning to strike a blow, a hammer-blow, against all the injustices of the world. He stood up and drained his glass. "We'll see about that," he said.

The bully was leaning against the wall near the entranceway. He sprang forward when, in front of Mike, the panhandler scuttled out.

Mike grabbed the man by the throat. It was like touching an electric eel. Writhing, spitting, cursing hoarsely, the bully flailed his arms and lashed at Mike with several vicious kicks. One of his punches landed and the jagged edges of a ring opened a cut below Mike's left eye. At the sting of it, Mike went berserk. He thrust his thumbs into the bully's thorax and pressed until the flailing arms went limp and the man's face began to purple.

"Are you listening?" Mike rasped, kneeing hard into the man's groin. The man, his eyes bulging, nodded his head vigorously up and down. "All right, you sonofabitch, you leave my friend alone. If I hear you've been giving him a hard time I'm gonna come back and personally squeeze the shit out of you. Understand?" Mike shook him forcibly and again the man nodded, his eyes clouding with pain. "Good!" Mike said, and dropped him to the floor. The man lay huddled there, playing dead.

Mike looked around the room. It was silent except for the jukebox still belting out a tune. Everyone was standing, watching him. No one moved. A few of the men looked at Mike enviously. He was still young, still handsome, unquestionably the strongest man in the place.

Outside, the night was still warm but promising rain. The left side of Mike's face was throbbing and had begun to swell. He wiped a trickle of blood off his chin. The panhandler peered at the wound. "You're going to have a scar," he said. He spoke as if from a long distance in the past, with authority.

"Well, he won't bother you again," Mike said.

"I told him what I would do but he wouldn't believe me," the panhandler said. "Now he knows."

"Knows what?" Mike said, not really listening to the conversation, his body still shaking from the fight.

The panhandler looked up at him and then chose his words with care. "He knows," the panhandler said, "that I can always get some young guy to come back and have a drink with me."

"And do you think they'd fight for you?" Mike asked.

"You did."

MANDI

Her name was Mandi and, although only a guest at the wedding, she, not the bride, held court in the centre of the room. Tall, made taller by her high-heeled shoes, she nodded now at one, now at another of her retinue, smiled, laughed prettily, parried someone's sexual innuendo with an innuendo of her own, lifted an eyebrow, adjusted her dress, accepted another glass of sherry and permitted someone to light her cigarette.

As she did so, the large diamond on the fourth finger of her left hand glinted in the light over head.

"What an exquisite ring," exclaimed the bride whose name, unfortunately, was Samantha and who had just entered the room (having noticed that the party's centre of gravity - or levity, if you will - had shifted decisively away from her).

"Samantha!" Mandi beamed, holding out her arms for an embrace but not moving an inch in her direction. "You look simply stunning."

Samantha, an older woman marrying quickly for the second time, was so intent upon forging an alliance with her rival that it is unlikely she even noticed the distance she was being made to traverse. She was delighted to be joining Mandi's charmed circle and she made the most of her opportunity to become, again, the centre of attention of her own guests. She too held out her arms and taking rapid, mincing steps (all that the hem of her bright green bridal dress would allow), made small cooing noises of friendship as she came forward. But what began as a veritable rush and which should, if one's calculations of trajectory and velocity were correct, have resulted in the percussive explosion of a kiss, somehow defused itself and ended, instead, in the decorous brushing of each other's cheeks. In fact, a young man sitting by himself was surprised to observe that no makeup had been mussed and not a single strand of hair had gone astray.

"What a beautiful ring," Samantha said again, holding Mandi's left hand up to the light; and then, in a conspiratorial stage whisper: "It must be worth a fortune!"

Mandi smiled tactfully. Samantha, in spite of her name, was always so gauche; as if Mandi didn't realize that the reason Samantha was admiring the ring on Mandi's left hand was that it gave her a chance to display the gold band on her own. Of course, Samantha had done it cleverly. Mandi had to give her credit for that. Any moment now (if only Samantha would shut up) sheer politeness would oblige her to take notice of Samantha's wedding ring and thus, by implication, her married state (something which, as was about to be made manifest to all, still eluded Mandi's grasp).

"What a beautiful ring," Samantha twittered. "Did Edgar give it to you? Oh, don't tell me - you're engaged!"

Now that was really going too far. That was completely uncalled for. Samantha knew perfectly well (because Mandi had told her in strictest confidence) that Mandi was pregnant and that a proposal from Edgar was her most pious wish.

"And you look so trim!" Samantha enthused in her ear. "How do you do it?"

By way of answer, Mandi lifted her shawl away from her waist and did a tiny pirouette. There was no denying it, for a pregnant lady, she was remarkably trim.

She was also tired. Her retinue was breaking up. Samantha's babble, the interminable talk about jewellery and dieting, had (as Samantha no doubt intended) scattered even the most admiring of them. Samantha's new husband came up and, after a few perfunctory words, reminded her that she had to look after the rest of the guests. Samantha excused herself and her husband escorted her away, leaving Mandi alone and feeling ridiculous in the middle of the room. Worse, she had an empty sherry glass in her hand and no one was offering to refill it.

She sought refuge on a sofa, which was occupied, at the far end, by a young man wearing unfashionably long hair and an outlandishly loud Scottish tartan that had been made into a vest. Fortunately, he began the ritual of polite conversation by offering to get her a drink. In due course she discovered that he was half Jewish and half Scottish (which explained the loud tartan) and a little more prying revealed that he was a student of philosophy who, temporarily, was working as a janitor. She, it turned out, was a free-lance designer who, also temporarily she gave him to understand, was living with a man she did not love by the name of Edgar.

True, the young man was half her age (if one could believe that she was thirty-eight), but his youthful ardour seemed to attract her. His eyes told her how very much he admired her and so she believed him when his lips said the same. It was true that her skin looked radiant that evening (she would have to be careful about what light she let him see her in) and he, seeing her moisten her lips, assumed that she was nervous and therefore thinking about him.

"My name is Michael," he said after they had spoken for half an hour.

"Mandi," she said, "I spell it with an i."

"How interesting," he said, taken aback by the affectation but then forgiving her immediately. For wasn't it precisely the theatre of her that had attracted him: the melodramatic hat and veil, the high-heeled shoes, the studied grace with which she moved, the mascara, the perfume? Of course it was all self-conscious and artificial, an illusion. But somehow it seemed to prove that whatever she did not reveal must be very, very real.

"Who," said Michael to his hostess after everyone else had left, "is Mandi?"

He had been helping her with the dishes and the question caught Samantha in the middle of rinsing a cup.

"There must be an echo in here," she said. "Not twenty minutes ago, Mandi asked me the same thing about you."

She suddenly remembered the cup and finished rinsing it. When she handed it to him to dry, she used the opportunity to look at his features more closely. He was large and his blue eyes were attractive, and he had a sensuous mouth, but he was no movie star. Besides, he was far too young. She wondered what Mandi could possibly have seen in him. If anything, he looked remarkably like the man Mandi was already with.

"Well, what did you say?" he asked, losing his patience.

"Oh you know, the usual thing. Nothing much. I said you were sensitive and very young and that you liked reading books a lot and-"

She stopped. Michael was angrily gouging his dish towel into the empty eye of the coffee cup.

"Be careful," she said. "That's my best china."

He put it down and leaned against the counter with his back against his hands.

"I know she's living with someone, if that's what you're worried about," he said.

"You're not her type."

"You'd never know it from the way she was looking at me. What's her type?"

"Rich."

"Maybe she thinks I have a future."

"The future, as far as Mandi is concerned, couldn't come fast enough. Look, I shouldn't tell you this, but Mandi is pregnant and the man she's living with is on the verge of asking her to marry him."

"And you think I'll louse it up?"

"I think that's a reasonable assumption, don't you?"

She came to him in a dream that evening. She said nothing; merely opened the door to his small room and stepped in. He rose up on one elbow and was about to get out of bed to greet her in the semi-dark when he saw her gesture to be still.

Advancing slowly, she found the chair beside his small table and stood there taking off her clothes. He heard the rustle of her shawl, the fall of her dress as it ran down the length of her body and he saw her, white-golden and mysterious, as she stepped off the black half-shell her clothes had made in the middle of the floor...

Never a sound sleeper, he awoke before she reached his bed. Cursing his luck, he lit a cigarette and watched the glow at the end of it for a long time.

The bathroom was the only room in the house Mandi could truly call her own. She had talked Edgar into letting her re-do it back in the days when she only came to visit but invariably stayed the night. The issue had been a test, not just of Edgar's wealth - she knew already he was wealthy; Mr. Right, her mother might have said - but of his generosity. No man spends $50 000 on a bathroom unless his intentions are honourable. And Edgar, at nearly sixty, was honourable, there was no question about that.

But they were both getting older, there was no question about that either. His desire had begun to flag; he came to her apartment less and less often and when he did he was usually drunk and somewhat abusive. His once handsome salt-and-pepper hair looked increasingly like birdshit - another of her mother's favourite expressions - and his large blue eyes looked even larger behind the thickening glasses he was forced to wear. She began to sense he

24

was dissatisfied, not just with her, but with himself, and that, in a man, is a very dangerous thing. She would have to act quickly or she would find herself replaced. No one is indispensable, she reminded herself, but some people are more difficult to get rid of than others.

Hence the bathroom. A delaying tactic, admittedly; at worst, a chance to play mistress in both senses of the word in the twenty-seven-room monstrosity he called his home. But a foot in the door nonetheless. After all, who but she had the taste and inclination to oversee the details of construction and decor - the choice of drapes and rugs, the gold-plated faucets, the placement of the plants (practically a forest of ficus and ornamental palms) and the hand-painted Venetian tiles that marched their ranks up a series of steps to the splendour of the solid marble bath?

Inevitably, he had been forced to give her a set of keys - only to be harried out of the house by the tramp of jack-booted workmen and the inescapable perfumes of plaster and paint. In the evening, across the dinner table, she would describe the progress of her handiwork and show him pictures culled from a thousand magazines.

"Do you like this urn? I thought it would look perfect beside the door.

"What do you thing of this volute?

"Really, I'm not satisfied with the choice of rug. I think something more ethnic would be better, don't you?"

Slowly the room filled up with vases and vials and volutes and objects made of Roman glass until the eight full-length mirrors reflected the gradual tightening of Edgar's once-sensuous mouth and the silent outrage of the single bald spot in the middle of his hair. There was something perverse about the way she slept with her make-up on, without moving, lying on her back all night so as not to mess it or disturb the falls she wore pinned in her hair.

He began hinting that it was time for her to leave.

The cellulite treatment hadn't worked, that was the problem. She sat on the clean white marble of the commode and surveyed the damage it had done to her upper thighs. No wonder Edgar had practically stopped making love to her - he could feel the lumps no matter how carefully she kept her nightdress on and never let him see.

She wiped herself - not in a dainty way, but methodically, conscientiously, as befitted the daughter of a nurse - and then washed herself thoroughly in the bidet. Her period was definitely over. In a few days, Edgar would have to go away on business for a week. The timing couldn't be better: the weekend would see her at the peak of her cycle - important because he had definitely asked her to leave and she had cried and had told him she was pregnant.

It was a good lie - amazing how it had come to her lips spontaneously - the ultimate female weapon. But she had seen the look of panic in Edgar's eyes and knew it was the angle she needed. Of course, he would squirm a little on the hook but even he knew he was beaten. There were too many witnesses: the workmen who had seen her at all hours in her bathrobe; the tradesmen who had sold her all those vases and vials and volutes; the friends Edgar had made the mistake of asking her to entertain. (She had told them, of course, as quickly as she could. The women were especially helpful; they made sympathetic noises and gave her post-partum advice and immediately told their husbands, lovers and friends - which was the point of it all.) No, Edgar could be counted on not to fight. He too would make the appropriate noises (he was already listening to the rumblings of her stomach with an attentive ear.) He would do the right thing.

The only unfortunate aspect of the situation was that, sooner or later, she would have to deliver. She could see her body in the full-length mirrors - the back, the front, the sides - and she thought of it bloated with child, the stretch marks afterward, the spongy mess her belly would become when the flesh collapsed like fallen dough.

Pregnancy, disfigurement - the very things she had guarded against all her menstrual life. She thought of the abortions she had had. Sometimes it seemed as if her whole life had been a constant battle, a never-ending pruning of a plant that, having flowered so beautifully, stupidly insisted on going to seed. And then, when she finally wanted to be pregnant, needed to be pregnant, she couldn't get the man she wanted to come across; had actually been forced to find, had already found, in fact, a substitute. It was a gamble but the young man looked enough alike.

It was the disfigurement that really bothered her. She consoled herself with the thought that she could have a preemie by Caesarean; she was sure the scar could be concealed. (She would have to check it out with Dr. Shoggi in the morning.) Certainly, she had no fear of the surgeon's knife. In the course of perfecting and then preserving her body she had experienced the scalpel many times. Aside from the abortions, her nose had been done (she had opted for a snub-nosed, pretty one - a tragic mistake given how the fashion later changed) and a piece of bone had been added to her chin. Bags of silicone had been implanted in her breasts and her derriere had been surgically lifted not two weeks after she had overheard someone at a party say it looked like a drop-leaf table.

No, she had no illusions about her body. Men did - that was the difference. She could look at herself in the full-length mirrors, see the grub-white skin around her waist, the muscle flabby through lack of exercise, and not blink an eye. She thought of her internal organs, the pancreas, the pyloric valve, the lungs, the egg making its strange journey from ovary to womb. She thought of Michael that weekend and of how she would explain to Edgar, when the time came, that the baby was overdue.

Michael was intimidated in the large four - poster bed; on the underside of its canopied ceiling a wounded white unicorn was surrounded by medieval knights and from all four sides some sort of flowered lace or muslin hung down to the floor. He lay on his elbow not daring to move. Although it was already morning, the light which filtered in through the curtain left the interior of the bed still semi-dark; he could barely make out Mandi's profile where she lay face-up on the satin pillow. He was relieved to notice that her breathing was shallow but regular, broken only now and then by a thin, high whistle in her nose.

He himself had slept fitfully, tormented by the twin agonies of shame and claustrophobia. He felt that he had failed miserably. He remembered how, playing for time, he had lingered over her breasts and done his best to ignore the imperious triangular patch between her thighs until, growing impatient, she had slithered her body beneath his own and learned the nature of his problem.

"I guess I'm over-eager," he had lied. She was still for a moment and then he had felt her hand, at first methodically but in the end desperately, stroking him up and down.

No effect.

Of course she had been understanding; disappointed perhaps, exasperated, but understanding.

"Don't worry," she had said. "It happens to everyone now and then."

He thought of the white chesterfield in the all-white room where, earlier that evening, she had served him black coffee in matching white cups; if he had not put milk and sugar in it, he would have ruined the decor. She had spoken of decor. A white cat had eyed them from the middle distance of the white rectangular rug. When it meowed and jumped up between them, he discovered it had been declawed.

"I'll do better in the morning," he promised.

She kissed him for his bravado. "We've got the whole weekend," she had said.

His problem was that he couldn't breathe, had been unable to breathe, in fact, since she had shown him the bathroom and the four-poster bed.

"Astonishing," he said when he saw the forest of ficus and the ornamental palms.

"That's what the reporter from *Architectural Digest* said too. They're going to do a full-colour spread. Do you like the carpet?"

"Very much." It was the only thing in the room he actually liked. "What is it? Navajo?"

"Why, yes. How did you know? I wanted something really ethnic to accentuate the - "

Michael had bent over double and was inspecting something n the carpet very intently.

"What are you looking for?" she asked.

"I'm looking for the flaw."

"Flaw?" she bristled. "What makes you think there's a flaw?"

"There always is." Michael was peering even more intently. "There, there it is. See where the pattern should be red but instead it's black?"

Mandi was shocked. "Should I get it replaced?"

Michael laughed. "No, you don't understand," he said. "The Navajos do it on purpose."

"But why?"

"Because they believe that a perfect carpet would trap the gods inside. They put the flaws there on purpose to let the gods escape. The Persians do the same thing, by the way, but for different reasons. They're afraid of God's jealous wrath."

"How do you know so much," she asked, "about decor?" She was impressed. She moved closer. There was no honourable way out; no way he could leave without insulting her. He gave her a kiss and began to unbutton her blouse. Perhaps, if they had made love, just then, on the carpet, everything would have been all right. But Mandi had been afraid of the bathroom's revealing light and had led him instead to the four-poster bed.

Luckily, the mattress was a good one. It barely moved as he lifted the curtain and stepped onto the floor. His clothes lay where he had felt compelled to fold them, neatly draped across the back of a nearby chair. He began to dress. Mandi shifted uneasily. He held his breath. When he heard her high, thin whistle, he put his shoes on, and left.

THE ACCIDENT

He had lost his job, not that it mattered except that his money was running low and somewhere inside he felt the loss of self-esteem. It bothered him that the other stations he had tried either didn't like his voice or his "arty" patter or the fact that he had told his last boss where to go.

Out of habit, he still got up at eight, washed his face, shaved, listened to the news - some other poor bastard reading someone else's lines. He himself had other things to do. He had free time and, except when he was feeling lonely, he was thankful. He could write or, if he felt like it, go for a walk. If he was lucky, the mailman might even shove one his rejected manuscripts through the slot. He had no personal correspondence. His mother - his father had long ago given up - wrote him once a month. Hers was a disciplined love, like her handwriting and the way she signed herself "Mother" - a statement of fact if not inclination.

She said she was disappointed that his engagement had broken off. He thought of her blue-veined, spotted hands, the wedding ring sitting loosely on the wizened interval between knuckle and joint. She would never understand.

Nor could he explain those coloured bits of paper he sometimes got, unpostmarked, at irregular times, from some female admirer - he had no idea who. And yet they came, shoved under his door or into the slot, always when he wasn't home. Whoever it was she was obviously keeping watch. He could not even be sure it was a she, although he thought it was because he could not imagine a man cutting hearts and flowers out of magazines along with the words, "Be My Valentine" and "Graham Turner, I Love You."

Of course, he was intrigued. Hearing footsteps at his door, he had several times jerked it open only to reveal his empty landing or one or another of his neighbours going up or down the stairs. Not wanting to appear nosy, he had then been forced to continue his motion, closing the door behind him and going out, although it was cold outside and he hadn't worn his coat. And once he had made a great show of leaving, had walked up Yonge Street slowly and then hurried back via back streets and re-entered his building by the rear. He had sat by his door all morning, not moving. But no one came that day nor for the rest of the week. The next note he got showed a broken heart and the words, "It's Not Fair To Peek."

———

He was in the midst of his routine when the mailman shoved a manuscript through the slot. He carried its bruised and broken body back to his desk and slit it with a knife. Instead of the usual rejection slip, there was a letter from the editor and Graham began to read.

Dear Mr. Turner:

Enclosed please find your ms., entitled *The Engagement*, herewith returned.

I regret to say that we find your plots unsuitable for our magazine. In *The Engagement*, I note, the hero breaks off his affair with the heroine because he feels her love has sullied him. And yet the heroine is invariably described as beautiful, intelligent, virtuous, etc. What else does the man want? It just won't wash.

May I suggest, in closing, that romantic dilemmas of this kind belong to the fiction of an earlier age. Even your prose style smacks of--

The phone rang. It was a woman's voice, muffled and obviously disguised. "Graham," she said. "Graham." And hung up.

———

Arnold Drexler, the director, was sitting cross-legged atop his desk in the middle of the room. He was casting roles for his remake of the Book of Genesis, and Graham, who made a little money as an extra now and then, was auditioning for the part of Cain.

"I do wish you'd worn your three-piece suit," Drexler complained.

"To play Cain?" Graham was mystified.

"Didn't your agent tell you this was a Genesis in modern dress?"

"Yes, but I--"

"Well, never mind."

"I live just across the street," Graham offered. "I could get changed and be back in two minutes."

"That won't be necessary. We can pretend you're wearing a three-piece suit just as well, can't we?"

"Yes, of course." Graham understood that this was the sort of challenge an actor is expected to respond to with enthusiasm.

"I must say you have a very resonant voice," Drexler continued.

"I used to be a radio announcer," Graham cut in.

"And a fine English head. Very George the Fifth. Very nice, A little soft in the belly too, I see. Very nice. Now, go over to the window and keep your back to me. This is a mime scene and I want to see you outlined against the light."

Graham did as he was told and, much to his surprise, found himself staring into the windows of this own apartment opposite.

"Now, imagine you're standing with Abel," Drexler went on. "He's directly in front of you. You see a stick lying in the mud. You pick it up. Slowly. More slowly. That's it, stealthily. This is your chance. You lift the club and you--"

Graham was standing with an imaginary club held high in his right hand. Down below, someone was emerging from the front door of his apartment building. She seemed to be nervous and, before stepping out, she checked the street carefully and then turned quickly to her right.

"No, no, no!" Drexler shouted. "You don't just stand there. You bring the stick down with one hard blow!"

You know my name?
Yes, I do.
You know who I am?
Yes, I do.
And you want me?

Yes, I do.
You want to make love to me?
Yes, I do.
You want to make love to me?
Yes, I do.
And you remember me?
Yes, I do. We were in high school together. I remember we lay naked one summer afternoon and you had soft golden skin.
I was a virgin.
I remember we were lying in your parents' bed. You were on your stomach and I went inside your rear end. You looked at me over your shoulder.
I was frightened.
You looked surprised. I thought you looked surprised.
You came then.
I know. I couldn't help myself.
I felt it burning inside.
You just lay there while I got the Kleenex. You didn't say anything.
I was frightened. You were so passionate. It frightened me.
The point is--

The phone rang. He stopped writing.
"Hello, Melanie," he said. There was a long pause and then the slow expulsion of breath.
"You guessed."
"I saw you. I was in a window across the street."
She paused again and then gave a small nervous laugh. "You must think I'm crazy."
"Definitely."
"Do you mind?"
"I'm flattered."
It was his smoothest voice. It pleased him to hear her nervousness.
"Would you like to see me sometime?" she asked.
He pretended to think it over. He took his time. "Sure," he replied.
"How about this evening?" she suggested.
"This evening would be fine."

———

And yet, by the time he reached her apartment, he realized he had given in. His loneliness had gotten the better of him. He had agreed to become entangled in a fantasy - but whose fantasy? He felt resentful and less sure of himself. What were his motives, anyway? Did he expect, when she opened the door, to find innocence? Did he really expect to find a seventeen-year-old girl with a laughing animal smile and no memories?

And what was she expecting? The bookworm she had known when she was a cheerleader and they had lain together one sweaty summer afternoon? Obviously not. After all, she had been watching him, stalking him, for months, perhaps even years for all he knew.

"Can I take your coat?"

They stood staring at each other. He noticed she did not look surprised or disappointed. He hoped he did not look surprised or disappointed.

"It's good to see you again," he said.

She coloured and put his coat on a hook behind the door. "You too," she said, her voice muffled by her back. Then, overcoming her shyness, she turned around and asked, "Can I get you some tea?"

"That would be very nice."

She had put on weight. Her face was pudgy. She was wearing a loose-fitting smock which obliterated the outlines of her figure. He looked about for a chair.

"I'm afraid we'll have to sit on the floor," she said, indicating a low, round table in the middle of the square carpet.

"I'll just look around the room," he said.

She disappeared into the kitchenette and he tried to surmise something about her by the way she lived. The apartment was small and furnished in a way which reminded him of the Sixties. Aside from the low table with its mandatory candlestick, ashtray and incense, an Indian bedspread hung across the ceiling. A bookshelf featured the Kama Sutra and the Upanishads and the Tibetan Book of the Dead, also several first-year university texts on psychology and literature. A television set was propped on a bureau at the foot of the bed - no doubt, he thought, the flickering witness to many a lonely orgy. A sudden wariness seized him. He went over to the bed and pulled back the sheets, running his quivering fingers under the pillows.

"What are you doing?" She was standing in the doorway of the kitchenette with two mugs and a teapot in her hands.

Graham whirled. "I was just testing the bed," he said lamely. It sounded ridiculous.

She bent her head with acceptance, put the tea things on the table and sat down. "Aren't you," she asked matter-of-factly, "rushing things a bit?"

"Actually, I was looking for a knife."

She looked at him wide-eyed for a moment, then threw her head back and laughed. "And I thought I was crazy!"

Graham stood stupidly in the centre of the room.

"I'm sorry," she said. "I didn't mean to embarrass you."

She patted the carpet beside her. Graham sat down and crossed his legs with difficulty. Melanie poured him his tea. "Tell me," he said in an effort to regain some semblance of superiority, "what happened to you after high school."

"I did some modelling," she said. "And then I got married." She looked at him with a rueful smile. "And then I got divorced."

Graham nodded but said nothing. He made it clear that he expected more.

"Well, I was in an accident, you know..."

"What accident?"

"I was in a head-on collision. I was clinically dead."

Graham shook his head sympathetically. Absorbed in what Melanie was saying, he had straightened his legs and was now leaning much closer to her on his elbow. Melanie touched his arm.

"I was in a bodycast for a year. Flat on my back. I put on weight. That's when my husband left. I'm afraid I'm not as pretty as I used to be."

"You mean when you were seventeen."

"Yes."

She lay on the carpet. Her hand tugged at him.

"I work in a cancer ward," she said. "It's mostly old men. They call me the Angel of Death."

Graham excused himself. The bathroom, she told him, was next to the kitchenette. His penis was throbbing when he took it out. There were no thoughts in his head. He inventoried the room: a cake of discoloured soap, a single toothbrush, bottles of aspirin and perfume, a container of Saniflush. Pinned on the wall opposite the toilet was a full-length poster of a bare-chested man whose face was remarkably like his own.

"I'm over here," she called when he re-entered the room. He already knew she would be lying on her stomach in the bed. The candle on the table gave the only light. He went over to her and undressed. When he lifted the sheets, he saw the pale expanse of her back, her buttocks, the shadowy cleft inviting him in. He kissed her shoulder and eased himself between her legs.

"Is it nice?" she asked.

Graham closed his eyes. "Yes, it is."

His hands curled around her body and embraced her breasts. But, then, when his fingers slid lower along her belly, he felt something warm and rubbery against her abdomen. His fingers stiffened.

"Don't worry," she said. "It's from the accident. It won't break."

"I'm sorry," he said. He kissed her neck apologetically, tenderly, and then, after a decent interval, went back to fondling her breasts.

DINNER WITH STALIN

Only once have I been told I look like someone else - a man who stripped at a peace rally and marched three-legged down the city street. The friend who saw "me" do it believed I actually had - there was a note of surprised respect in his voice - and, frankly, I've felt myself a changed man ever since: more dashing, more courageous, a man capable of wild and unpredictable things.

So, sitting down at the restaurant table across from Victor Gant - "Vic to his friends," he assured me as we all shook hands and Sandra introduced him to my girlfriend April and myself - I wondered whether he too had been affected, whether he had been changed in any way, by his remarkable resemblance to the late dictator and mass-murderer, Joseph Stalin.

Do I need to describe him - Victor, I mean? He had the same handsome, cunning forehead rising to the same thick blue-black hair cowled with a slick of grey; the same eyebrows; the same swarthy skin; the same thick moustache hiding dark, sensuous lips; the same dog-white teeth. No, we all know Victor's face - it's features stamped in our minds by a thousand photographs and documentary films.

But I do want to describe his eyes. No photograph could capture the look in them - the kindly, soft, brown, thoughtful, appraising, intense, playful, cold, cruel, lifeless, shifty, frightened look in them. I tell you, I had dinner with a man named Victor Gant but, for an hour and a half, I stared into the eyes of Joseph Stalin.

Sandra said, "I'm so glad you two've finally met. You've so much in common. I just know you'll be friends."

Sandra and I worked at the bank. Sandra was the office manager. I was the new VP Marketing, enjoying the money, the prestige and the power. It was the prestige that most went to my head. After years of living alone in a room writing a novel which, when finally published, sold 287 copies, I had needed some sort of worldly success to patch the tattered flag of my self-respect. So I revelled in the big deals in the big office with the big desk. And when I shook hands with Victor Gant - Stalin or no Stalin - it was with the hearty, haughty indifference of a senior executive magnanimously deigning to dine with the boyfriend of an underling.

At least, that was the impression I was trying to give. Actually, I felt ill at ease because the attractive young lady smiling and shaking hands beside me, my girlfriend April, was Sandra's secretary. So Sandra had me by the short and curlies and she knew it. Worse, she knew I was a writer. That is why, over the past several months, she had developed the disconcerting habit of walking into my office and unburdening her soul.

At first she had talked about Dave. Dave was her husband. Dave used to be in the army but now worked as a security guard. Dave liked to go bowling. Dave did not like to read books. Dave had tattoos on his arms. She could not take Dave to parties. She was not happy with Dave.

Then she began talking about Vic. Vic was intellectual. Vic gave her books - in particular, *The Virtue of Selfishness*, by Ayn Rand. Under Vic's tutelage, she told me, she had come to feel that her social and mental horizons were being unduly cramped by her marriage; it was her duty, her moral duty, to be selfish - really, the book had been a revelation. For a month or so she called Vic her soul-brother; they were strictly platonic, she assured me. Then, suddenly, she was living with Vic and there was an ugly scene at the bank when Dave tried to force his way in to see her - unsuccessfully, of course, because there are guards at a bank - followed by phone calls: a man claiming to represent a credit agency wanting to know Sandra's new home address and phone number.

And one day Sandra walked into my office and closed the door and burst into tears. Dave knew she was living with someone but he did not suspect Vic. He did not suspect Vic because Vic was, and still remained, Dave's best friend...

"I've heard a lot about you," Victor said.

I've always disliked that line as an opening gambit because it puts the other person on the defensive. True to form, I felt defensive.

"Likewise," I replied. I lifted an eyebrow to suggest that I, too, knew more than I cared to say. "I hear you are a great fan of Ayn Rand."

"Oh, isn't she just fantastic?" Sandra piped in excitedly, her hand clutching my forearm. "I'm reading *The Fountainhead* right now. Vic says the next book I have to read is *Atlas Shrugged.*"

"I see you have a mentor," I observed, dodging her question, astonished that Victor had taken her over so completely.

Victor looked at me, the expression in his eyes impish, imperious. "What do you think?" he asked.

"About what?"

"About Ayn Rand."

I leaned back in my chair, conscious that my understated banker's blue contrasted well with his flashy grey silk and the gold bracelet ostentatiously chained around his wrist.

"Well, I think she's done an excellent job of popularizing Nietzsche's main ideas. Unfortunately, in the process, I'm afraid some of the subtlety has been lost."

There! I had put Victor firmly in his place. No more upstart remarks from that quarter. I noticed a flicker of doubt cross Sandra's face. April gazed at me lovingly.

And then Victor did something I did not expect. His lips parted and a broad, toothy, delighted smile flashed beneath his black moustache. He shook his head. Still smiling, he turned to Sandra, jerked a thumb in my direction and said, "You know, I really like this guy."

Sandra beamed at me. The waitress came and we ordered drinks. I was pleased to see the way she automatically assumed I was the head of the table. Victor eyed her backside as she walked away and Sandra slapped his arm playfully. We studied the menus, ordered, ordered more drinks, made small talk and I thought the dinner was going pleasantly enough when I made the mistake of asking Victor what line of business he was in.

"I run a collection agency," he said. "If somebody owes somebody money, I put the squeeze on him."

I said, thinking vaguely that Victor was probably angling for a job with the bank, "Of course, you charge a fee."

"Twenty-five percent of the debt, up front."

"What if you don't collect?"

Stalin's eyes glinted.

"I always collect."

I laughed. He laughed. We all laughed.

"Oh, come off it," I said.

Stalin's shoulders gave a Slavic shrug. "I was an interrogator in Nam. Believe me, there's always a way, always some place where a man is weak."

"Oh, come off it," I said again, rather stupidly I thought. Was I imagining things, or had Victor's words, very, very subtly, been intended as a challenge - to me? I glanced at April and thought that she, too, had stiffened. I felt Victor's eyes on me and, for a moment, dared not look up. I sensed him probing, seeking out that weak spot in my psyche into which he could plunge his interrogator's needle or electrode or whatever the latest instrument of torture might be. I did not doubt, not at all, the truth of his having been an interrogator in Viet Nam. Nevertheless, I felt I had to taunt him, take him down a peg with a quip.

"You mean you never met a sucker you couldn't break?"

Now he stiffened. There was a pause. Then he leaned forward and our eyes caught and neither of us looked away.

"Never," he said bluntly.

We continued to stare at each other in silence. The tension mounted.

It is an axiom in business that the person who speaks first, after an offer has been made on a deal, loses. The same is true of blinking during a staring contest. But to go on staring at Victor was to admit him as an equal and to do that was, I felt, already to lose. My one chance was to seize the initiative. So I broke the stalemate and forfeited the round. I smiled as if this conversation we were having were merely a matter of idle philosophical speculation and said, "You know, you are talking to a man who has read Solzhenitsen's *Gulag Archipelago.* They tried to break him - they threw everything they had at him - but he never broke."

Stalin snorted triumphantly, contemptuously. "The Russians! Are you kidding? They're still living in the Middle Ages. They don't know a thing about modern methods. You give me Solzhenitsen for a couple of weeks and he'd be begging to become an informer for the KGB."

"Not if he's willing to die," I countered. "Not if he's reached the point where his dignity as a human being is more important to him than his eyes or his fingers or his life."

Stalin grinned, looked at Sandra, jerked his thumb in my direction. "He thinks I'm a torturer," he said incredulously. "He doesn't understand." He turned again to me. "I don't hurt people. I help them. These are people in a very difficult, very dangerous situation. These people are prisoners. I become their friend, their confidante, their trusted guide through the maze of their guilts, their fears, their obsessions. They confess because there's a bond between us, because they love me."

He spoke as though he were pleading with me, as though it were desperately important that I understand him and what he had done and everything he stood for. It was the plea of a proud, guilty, complex man for sympathy.

And, of course, it was a trick, part of the very technique he had just been describing.

"I don't think you could break me," I said.

"Give me half an hour."

"You couldn't break me because I wouldn't fall for your psychological bait-and-switch. I'd know exactly what you were doing. I know exactly what you are doing now."

Stalin's eyebrows lifted. His eyes were round with offended innocence. "What am I doing?" he wanted to know. He appealed to April and Sandra. "What am I doing?"

Sandra giggled nervously. April said, "I think we should change the subject."

"Yes," I said, signalling the waitress peremptorily. "Let's change the subject."

The waitress hurried over, cleared the few remaining dishes, brought fresh drinks.

"Fine!" Victor said. "What shall we talk about? Tell me," he demanded, immediately answering his own question, "in 25 words or less, what is the code you live by, what is your philosophy of life?"

It was a rehearsed question, obviously another trick in his endless bag of tricks designed to throw the other person off balance. No doubt he had his own answer ready as well. But - was this the hook that caught me, that finally dragged me under his spell? Or had that already happened? When, exactly, had I chosen to enter into this contest of wills? And had I chosen? And was the contest my idea or his? - but, I couldn't help myself, I found the question intriguing. Besides, I was reasonably certain that if it came to matching philosophical wits, I would win.

"In 25 words or less?"

Victor leaned back in his chair and, smiling inscrutably, waited.

"All right," I said theatrically. "I'll give you an answer that combines both the Jewish and the Greek sides of our heritage. I give you Rabbi Hillel and Socrates with one small word added by myself: 'Do not do unto others that which you would not have them do unto you.' And, 'The unexamined, *undignified* life is not worth living.'"

Victor counted out the words on his fingers. "That's 23 words," he said. "I'm impressed. I'm very impressed." He lifted his drink, saluted me, drained it, ordered another round before I could protest. "I'm really very impressed," he said again, nodding his head sagely as if confiding his admiration to no one but himself.

I did my best *Gone With The Wind* Clark Gable imitation: "'Frankly, my dear, I don't give a damn.' I don't give a damn if you're impressed or not."

Stalin's smile collapsed, the portcullis of his moustache closed over the dog-white teeth. His eyes narrowed and pondered me shrewdly, amusedly. Finally he said, "You're lying."

He said it slowly, confidently. He turned to Sandra. "He's lying. He's lying to me."

"I am not lying!" I snapped, feeling at the same time, helplessly, that I had fallen into a trap.

He turned back to me and enunciated each word clearly and distinctly. "You are lying. You were trying to impress me - any fool can see that."

"All right," I admitted. "I'm lying."

Stalin slapped the table with his right hand. "This guy is fantastic!" he shouted. A delighted grin creased his face. He stood up and quickly came around the table. "You're beautiful," he said. He stretched his arms out drunkenly. "Let me give you a hug."

He leaned forward. His hands clasped my shoulders and began pulling me towards his chest. I straight-armed the side of his neck.

"But we understand each other," he said. "You're not really a banker, you're a writer. I'm an interrogator. We're not like other people. Come, let us seal our friendship. Give me an embrace."

I continued, grimly, to hold him at arm's length. He pulled at my shoulders. His face leaned very near.

"It takes two to embrace," I answered. "Both have to agree to the time and place." I gave him a final shove away.

Stalin looked hurt, disappointed. "Hey!" he laughed, recovering and returning to his seat. "He really is a writer. He's a poet and don't know it. *It takes two to embrace/Both have to agree to the time and place.* Not bad. Not bad."

He waggled his head appreciatively and took another long pull on his drink.

"And you?" I asked, pressing home my advantage. "What's your philosophy - in 25 words or less?"

He set down his drink, put his elbows on the table and pursed his lips.

"My philosophy of life is this: Do good to your friends and fuck your enemies - that's my philosophy."

"Oh, Victor!" Sandra hissed. She tried to put a restraining hand on his arm but he brushed it aside impatiently.

"That's my philosophy and it's a hell of a lot more honest than that bullshit you spewed out at me. Let me--"

"No, you let me," I interrupted. April was fidgeting, a clear sign she wanted to leave, but I had the moral high ground and, this time, I was not going to let him outflank me. "I'm sorry, Sandra, but I can't believe I'm hearing this crap about honesty from a man who's sleeping with the wife of his best friend."

Victor's fist slammed the table-end and he half rose from his seat. "You don't know Dave," he raged. "He's mentally unstable. He was in Nam with me. I know what I'm talking about. He could seriously hurt Sandra." He sank back into his seat self-consciously. "This way, I know his every move. I know what he's thinking, what he's planning to do. I even suggest things. That business about the credit check, that was--"

He caught himself but it was too late. I had hit a nerve and he had made an explanation. I got to my feet. As I expected, April got up with me.

"I'm sorry, Sandra," I said, "but it was my duty to speak the truth. I really think you and Victor ought to sit down with Dave and make a clean breast of the whole thing."

Victor stared up at me with open-mouthed, mock astonishment. "You're good," he said admiringly. "You're really good. I loved that 'I'm sorry, Sandra' bit. That was a real good touch." He waggled his head to show his appreciation, sighed, stood up. Sandra slid out from behind the table and stood beside him. "Anyway, you had me going there for a minute." He held out his hand in a bravado show of good-sportsmanship and we shook on it.

"I'll take that embrace now," I said. I felt his hand jerk back reflexively but then - I could see it in his eyes - he realized he could not escape. He had offered the hug to me. His only hope was to outdo me.

He smiled broadly and opened his arms wide. I felt the powerful muscles of his chest when we clinched. "Have you ever been kissed by a man?" he asked suddenly. And then I felt myself being pulled towards his black moustache and his dark, parted lips.

"Never!" I cried and pressed my lips against his. I held him longer than he wanted. I felt him struggling to gain release.

I hugged him harder and stuck my tongue into the wetness of his mouth.

ERIC

It occurred to me, when my wife April phoned and told me that Eric had been arrested at Toronto's international airport for smuggling cocaine, that what little I knew of Eric Blackburn's life might make an interesting character study if I found time to write it. I make my living as a banker and, while it may be that I meet many intriguing types in the course of a day, I seldom get to know them well - it not being customary to reveal one's secret self to a banker while negotiating a loan. But Eric was so flamboyant, so disarmingly garrulous that, after I had opened an account for him, instead of the usual peremptory business directives he sent me a stream of long and confidential letters - letters which April read avidly and which eventually resulted in our accepting his invitation to visit him in Greece. It was only at the end of our stay in Greece that I realized how thoroughly we had been taken in: that he, who pretended to be a cultured man of eccentric charm and wit, was, in fact, that saddest of all human possibilities - a disappointed narcissist, an aging con man who had turned to selling dope.

"Is he in jail?" I asked.

"Yes," April said. She was crying. She still believed that Eric was unique, a frail bird of paradise who had somehow flown out of Eden and landed in the middle of the industrial twentieth century.

"Well, he knew the risks."

"But, Stephen, he's sixty years old!"

"Actually, by now, he's sixty-three."

"That's even worse. Steve--"

"April, forget it. There's nothing I can do."

"Why not?"

"Because they'll find out about Greece. They'll subpoena my records - the affidavit, his bank account, even his letters. I'm probably the worst witness against him."

"And you're not just a little bit worried about your reputation?"

"Of course I'm worried about my reputation. I'm worried they'll start thinking I'm his Toronto connection. I mean, maybe they'll think I'm Mr. Big or something. That's all I need."

In the end she went to visit him alone and came home depressed. They had led him in along with fifteen others and they had sat in a booth divided by bullet-proof glass, talking to each other by phone.

"He looked so old," April said. "He's got cancer of the skin."

"He told you that?"

"I could see the scar on his forehead! He's not a total phoney, you know."

"Maybe. But you said he told you the suitcase full of cocaine was a frame-up. You know damn well that's the same lie he told us in Greece."

"But he was pointing at the phone. He was afraid it was tapped. So of course he lied. He was talking for the record. What he said was, 'April, someone planted that stuff in my bag.' And then he must have seen the doubt in my eyes because that's when he pointed at the phone and said, 'Why would I lie? I could tell you that I did it because I didn't know what else to do. I could tell you I did it because I was old and sick and lonely and broke. But that wouldn't be true.' Don't you see, Stephen? He was talking between the lines."

"All right," I said. "But there's still nothing I can do."

She looked at me then with her frightened, questioning eyes. I held her like a child and she said how lucky we were to have found each other, over and over again.

I remember that when I first met Eric he came into my office wearing gloves and a dark mink coat which, when he opened it, revealed the most amazing red silk lining. He was handsome in a sandy, fine-boned way and I was struck by the elegance of the way he leaned back in the chair opposite my desk and casually crossed his legs.

"I would like to open an account," he said, "in the name of Marshall Lovejoy." Here he took off his gloves and folded them neatly in his lap.

"Well, uh, Mr. Lovejoy--"

"Marshall," he said.

"Well, uh, Marshall, I'm sure any of our tellers would be delighted to accommodate you."

"I'm sure," he said. "But I travel a great deal and there would have to be arrangements. You see, I have a villa abroad."

"I see. May I ask where?"

"In Greece. On the island of Lesbos made famous by Sappho as the island of love."

"That's where the word *lesbian* comes from, isn't it?"

He smiled at me then, his watchful eyes wrinkling with appreciation at having found someone - a banker of all people! - who knew such a thing. He allowed me to gather that he was impressed.

"I'm afraid it's become somewhat tacky since then," he confided, his smile turning downward at the corners a bit. "A lot of riff-raff, mostly writers like myself, artists, tourists, that sort of thing." The smile collapsed entirely at this, replaced by a look of petulant disdain.

"So you're a writer then," I went on, picking up the conversational nugget he had so carefully placed for me to find. He smiled again. His gambit was that since most people are impressed by writers, he would confound them further by affecting to look down on Mount Parnassus from some Olympian height.

"Among other things. I'm afraid I have a scholarly turn of mind. However, the account I wish to entrust you with is quite a sizeable one."

"Fine," I said. "How can we help?"

He grinned. Diffidently. It was really too amusing, the grin seemed to suggest, a harmless conspiracy between friends. Surely he could confide in me now that we had gotten to know each other so much better.

"Would there be any problem," he wanted to know, "if someone's name weren't actually Marshall Lovejoy?"

I learned later that his real name was Eric Blackburn, that he had grown up in Hollywood in the care of a widowed aunt and that he was related in some way to a famous actor. He himself had tried his hand at playing bit parts but nothing had come of this and he had drifted away to Europe and the Second World War. He once told me that, as an ambulance driver in Italy, he had saved the life of the Crown Prince and, while I never convinced myself that this was true, I gathered that he spent the fifties hobnobbing with the titled and the wealthy and, I suspect, living off their patronage. He must have seemed to them a dashing figure in his youth: handsome, as I said, a dreamer, a curiosity, a golden-haired American with enough culture to prefer the European, a free spirit beholden to no one except whoever was lucky enough for the moment to be his patron, a genuine Bohemian but with impeccably good manners, always discreet but always willing to tell again that amusing story about when Fellini owned a used car lot or how Salvador Dali drank before he met his wife.

The sixties had ushered in more of the same, only better: morals were loose, a steady job in disrepute - and everyone had an awful lot of money. Thousands of unwashed, idealistic youths - myself among them - made pilgrimages to Paris, Istanbul, Beirut, the Himalayas. Eric opened a nightclub in Katmandu. He married.

And then it was over. The youths stopped coming to Katmandu. They trickled back to their parents' homes, washed, shaved, exchanged their favourite koans for the names of a few good brokers, went into business. There was nothing left for Eric to do but sell his nightclub and move to Greece. His wife had left him to become a nun in a lamasery and the old elite was gone, swallowed by old age or an overdose or, like Fellini, by success.

As his bank account dwindled, his letters became longer. The winters, he wrote, had lately turned colder. He had to keep his shutters closed and his landlord (this is how I learned for the first time that he did not own the villa) refused to install central heat - a scandal, Eric said, because he had paid for it and the landlord was the mayor. In a few more days, if the weather did not turn warmer, he would be reduced, like the natives, to sitting huddled around fires of burning olive pits. Nevertheless, his villa, he said, would always have room for us or, as he put it: "I would be honoured if you and April were to come at the end of this summer and share with me the golden harvest of ancient Greece."

I cabled that April and I would arrive on August 22nd for a stay of three weeks.

He cabled back: "Under arrest. Not to worry. Come anyway."

He had arranged a sofa and a couple of worn but comfortable armchairs in the shade of a pendant lemon tree in the small walled garden which formed the courtyard of his villa. There, sitting in a faded kimono, one bluish leg thrown over the other at the knee, he told us that he had been arrested for possession of hashish.

Ridiculous, he said, because he had long ago outgrown that sort of thing. "And I can assure you," he added, "that if I had had some, it would not have been peeking out from under my bed." The police, he said, had gone straight to the spot. An obvious set-up."

"But who would want to frame you?" I asked.

"The mayor." He explained that he had recently re-rented the villa for five years and had paid in advance. He had also wanted major repairs - including central heat - and again he had paid in advance. "I trusted him," Eric continued defensively. "I've known the man for years. It never occurred to me that he would do such a thing - I mean, send me to prison? - just so he could pocket the money."

Out of the corner of my eye I could see that April was nodding her head sympathetically. Eric must have seen this too because he took her hand and patted the back of it.

"The truth is," Eric went on, "none of this would have happened if I hadn't befriended a young Greek soldier. We're only a few miles from the coast of Turkey, so there are soldiers billeted here. You can imagine their living conditions - appalling, I can assure you. I took pity on him. Andros, his name was. I remember thinking how noble he would have looked wearing a toga. He was a genetic throwback, no doubt about it - blond, curly hair, green eyes... At any rate, I invited him to my place, gave him a bath, cooked him a decent meal. I told him he could come and bathe any time he liked. My one rule was that he couldn't go upstairs.

"Well, to make a long story short, I came home one day and caught him coming our of my bedroom. He turned scarlet, of course, the minute he saw me and I should have suspected something right away. But he explained that he had been looking for a towel and I thought no more about it until that evening when the police came and went straight to the room. The rest, as they say, is history. I'm out on bail but I can't leave the island."

"How much did they find?" I asked.

Eric shrugged. "Five kilos."

"Five kilos!"

"In Greece, you know, hashish is very plentiful."

"How long could they put you away?"

"Seven years, give or take a few days."

April was angry, upset. "But Eric!" she cried. And then, turning to me, "Isn't there anything we can do?"

This, of course, was the opening Eric had been waiting for and I, I must confess, was gratified to see that, in a practical emergency, it was to me that April turned instinctively. Eric said: "You know, there is something. It's really my word against theirs. I've written to all my friends, Fellini, the Crown Prince -you know, I saved his life once during the Italian campaign - but do you think, now that I need a favour, that I can get even a character reference out of them?"

Somewhere, Eric's look of bewildered, injured pride seemed to suggest, a bomb had gone off. In the aftermath of the explosion, indifference, ingratitude and betrayal had engulfed the world.

"I could cable the bank and get them to notarize a statement," I offered. "I can testify that I've known you for years and that your business dealings and character have always been above reproach. How does that sound?"

He was deeply touched, profoundly moved, forever in my debt. He said that April didn't know how lucky she was, that perhaps I was a banker but I had the soul of a poet.

"Do you know what the name Stephen means?" he asked me.

"It's the name of an early Christian martyr, isn't it?"

"That's right, but it's also a flower, *Stephanotus*. In ancient Greece, during the Olympic games, alongside the sporting events they had contests between poets and dramatists. *Stephanotus* was the garland which crowned the winning poet's head."

"Well," I said. "I can see that I'd better get the lawyers working on that affidavit right away."

I would like to report that the rest of Eric's conversation, during the weeks that we waited for my affidavit to arrive, was equally fascinating and informative. But in this I was disappointed. At first I thought the fault lay with myself and therefore, one after the other, I tried politics, economics, sociology, anthropology, even, in final desperation, religion. No interest. I cudgelled my brains trying to remember books I had liked but either he had not read them or, if he felt he had to say that he had, he could not remember them either. Of course, he knew the authors in many cases - or at least he knew someone who knew them - but, aside from a few anecdotes, these discussions, I noticed, quickly degenerated into a species of vituperation: Kerouac had been a spunky kid but no Hemingway, while Hemingway was dismissed as a publicity-hound and a phoney; J.D. Salinger was a one-note-Johnny; Norman Mailer was too pushy and had sold out to journalism; Saul Bellow took himself too seriously, etc., etc. In short, western civilization had come to an abrupt end at approximately the same time that Eric had stopped reading.

He spent his days lying in bed or sitting, wrapped in his faded kimono, in his garden. He never went out or, if he did, it was only to accompany us to the market - the *agora*, as he invariably called it. He was a man under siege and we were his hostages - live-offerings might be the better word - to the surrounding hostile population. He introduced us to his friends Bernice and Azul: "This is Stephen, my banker, and April, his lovely wife." My title was supposed to impress but Azul merely smiled enigmatically and soon led Bernice away. Nevertheless, it was always "This is my banker" wherever we went and I came to realize that the words were a kind of talisman to frighten evil spirits - those dark shapes of old men and women who looked at us from behind their barred windows and who drew back into the shadows when we passed by.

But sometimes, in the evenings, he would talk about the places he had been and the strange customs he had seen. I recall, for example, the night he told us about his wife, how she had died of ordinary appendicitis in the lamasery and how monks had come from all over Tibet to witness her cremation. He had a photo of her in his bedroom - a high-cheekboned face with eyes staring at something beyond the camera. "I don't know how they did this," he said. "But after the flames had burned away her flesh, I could see that her bones were a vivid blue. Then they too burned away and there was nothing left but ashes."

He kept the photo in a special frame with two candle-holders attached to the bottom. It was a shrine and sometimes, when he thought we had gone to bed, we would see him slumped over his desk with the photograph in front of him and the candles burning.

———————

He warned us against going for walks because the island was mined. The soldiers had planted them against a Turkish invasion and then had lost the maps. A fisherman had been blown to bits just a few days before our arrival.

We went anyway. I remember I felt I had to get away from Eric's gangrenous negativity. We followed a path that climbed through a grove of olive trees and then out to a cemetery in a clearing where there seemed to be bees everywhere and the air was sickly-sweet with the smell of honey. April said:

"Are you in a snit?"

"No. Why?"

"You've hardly said a word."

"I'll be glad when we get home."

"Because of Eric?"

"Yes."

"Why?"

"Because there's something slowly rotting inside him."

"Well, I feel sorry for him!" April flared angrily. "I think it's beautiful the way he's still in love with his wife."

I mumbled something vaguely reassuring. Then we turned and walked back down the hill in silence.

The sun had already set by the time we returned to the villa. We found Eric waiting for us, grinning from ear to ear. The mailboat had arrived bringing my affidavit and a letter. He showed us the signature. It was from Frederico Fellini.

April looked at me triumphantly. Eric was exultant. "We should celebrate in the *agora*," he said. "Come, my dear friends, I'll buy the drinks."

He dressed with unusual flamboyance - even for him - in white slacks and jacket and long silk scarf. He was excited and kept asking April whether she approved his wide-brimmed hat as we made our way down the narrow streets to the tavern near the harbour.

It was a surprisingly chilly night, a harbinger of the coming Autumn - too cold to sit outside. When we opened the door we saw that the place was crowded with tourists and soldiers and fishermen and I thought we wouldn't be able to find a seat. But then Eric spotted Azul and Bernice. They were sitting at a table with a few of their friends and Eric shepherded us over to them.

I was struck, once again, by how coolly, even rudely, we were greeted. I wanted to leave but Eric insisted on us drawing up chairs and squeezing our way in. He showed everyone my affidavit and the letter from Fellini and introduced me as his banker all over again. When the oohs and aahs occasioned by Fellini's signature showed signs of faltering, he ordered drinks all around and a package of American cigarettes. These he opened and slapped down in the middle of the table.

He was smiling magnanimously and about to tell everyone to help themselves when his face froze. I saw that he was staring at a young man in an army uniform who had just come in. The young man stood leaning against the door, surveying the room and nodding now and then at someone he knew. His features, as Eric had said, were astonishing. He could have been Alcibiades, the one who fell in love with Socrates, or a reincarnation of Charmides, the youth whose beauty tempted all the men of Athens. He had the strangely feminine lips you see on statues of Alexander, the same straight nose, the same perfectly proportioned chin.

"Andros!" Eric said under his breath.

It was at that moment that the young man noticed Eric staring. A practiced leer spread across the young man's face and then, to my surprise, he put his thumb in his mouth and languorously sucked it in and out.

"Is that the one who framed you?" April asked.

But Eric had already left the table.

Bernice and Azul sniggered. "Nobody framed him," Azul said. He jerked his head in the general direction of the door where Andros, with a bemused smile, was watching Eric's pellmell scramble toward him. "Everyone knows what Eric used the stuff to pay for. One night a whole platoon of soldiers carried him naked through the streets."

April turned to me, her eyes frightened and questioning.

"Come on," I said quietly. "Let's go home."

WHEN JOHN GODFREY CAME TO

He hung back in the doorway with a stupid smile on his face while everyone chanted, "Come on, John, come on, read you poem." Then he gave in, holding the paper between thick, dirty fingers. When he finished, no one said anything. The roomful of people stared and he found himself smiling, exposing the stain where his tooth was chipped.

A small, bearded man said, "I don't like it." He was sitting with a thick manuscript on his knees, leaning against the chesterfield beside his girlfriend. "I don't like what it says and I don't like the rhythm."

John started folding his poem slowly, but then he crumpled it and threw it at the bearded fellow's chest.

"I write this thing from the heart," John shouted, "and you shit all over it?"

There were flecks of spit at the corners of his mouth. The other guests sat rigid.

"I didn't mean you should take it so personally," the bearded fellow said.

"What the fuck are you talking about? It's *my* poem, man!"

"I wasn't criticizing you, John."

John went into the kitchen and kicked the table. Then he kicked the table again and a knife fell onto the floor. He grabbed it and lunged back into the livingroom.

"Get up!" he ordered, kicking the bearded fellow's legs.

"John!" somebody cried. "This is the Peace House."

"I don't give a shit," John said. "I'm going to gut you like a fish." He jabbed the air above the bearded fellow's head. "I'm going to gut you like a fish," he repeated.

The manuscript was open on the bearded fellow's knees. "I was in the middle of a poem," he said. His tongue darted between his lips. "You get upset when someone criticizes your poem but now you won't even let me finish."

John hesitated. Then he went back to the doorway and stood there with the knife in his hand. "Okay," he said. "Finish it."

The bearded fellow looked at his girlfriend quickly. "It's a long poem," he sighed, "and now I'm going to have to start all over again."

"Just don't nobody try and leave," John said.

The bearded fellow flipped back to the beginning and began reading. Then he remembered that he hadn't read the title and began again. The title required a long explanation. So did the first line.

"Hurry up," John muttered. The speed was wearing off. He leaned against the doorjamb and slid down onto his haunches. The bearded fellow began another explanation. John's eyes were tired and he closed them. When he came to, he was lying on his back in the livingroom. Someone had plumped a pillow under his head.

"Anybody home?" he called.

There was no answer. John crawled towards the litter in the middle of the rug. One bottle still contained a little white wine and he used it to wash the medicinal taste of Captain Wonderful's speed out of his mouth. He drank a little more out of the bottom of a glass with lipstick on it and then he groped under the chesterfield and came out with the crumpled piece of paper:

I've got a plan
I've got a plan
I plan to kill a man
And the man I kill will
Be the one
Who gives me fun...

There were two more verses but he knew them by heart. He folded the paper neatly and put it into his wallet.

———

It was raining, a light drizzle. It was two or three in the morning and he pulled his blue raincoat close and walked across the Granville Street bridge. Occasionally a car's headlights shadowed him and he stuck his thumb out. No one gave him a lift.

Passing the Cloverleaf Hotel, a girl of about fifteen asked him if he wanted a good time.

"How much?" he asked.

"Fifty."

"You on junk?"

"What's it to you? You the man?"

"Do I look like the man?"

"You all look alike."

"Well, how much for a short time?"

"That *is* for a short time."

"You got to be kidding. Make it thirty."

"Okay," and she shrugged.

"You got a place?"

"The hotel."

"I ain't paying no hotel."

"So what, then?" she said. "You got a place?"

"How much," John said, "if you just give me head?"

The girl made a face and said it would cost the same. "Where?" she said.

"The men's room, in the hotel."

"The man'll kick us out," she said.

"Not if we don't go in together. He'll think you're going for a pee."

He started pulling her across the street. She held back. "You gotta give me the money first."

He gave her thirty dollars and she put it in the pocket of her jeans. The nightclerk hardly looked up. The toilets were downstairs, down a half flight of stairs. John checked out the Gents and said, "Okay," holding the door.

The girl slipped in and chose a stall. John locked the metal door. She knelt on the toilet seat so nobody coming in would see her legs. John stood in front of her and undid his pants. The girl spat on her hand and stroked him until he grew hard. After a while, John said, "I'm coming," and held her by the hair so she couldn't pull her head away. She was angry and reached for toilet paper. He thumped her on the back of the neck. He went through her pockets and found ninety dollars. He took eighty and left, lifting the collar of his coat so the nightclerk wouldn't get a good look at him.

The smell in his room was still unbearable. A few weeks earlier he had made a stew on his hotplate which he hadn't eaten. He lifted the lid and saw fuzzy green islands of scum floating on the surface. The thought of cleaning it, feeling the slime on his fingers, disgusted him. He took the pot off the hotplate and put it in his closet. Although it was cold, he opened a window.

The next day he scored some acid off Captain Wonderful and on his way home he bought a paper. The room didn't smell too bad but it was cold, so he got his into his cot fully clothed and covered himself with a blanket and his raincoat. The headline said some Turk had shot the Pope. Doctors were sure the Pope would live. John couldn't care less one way or the other, although he hated the guy who had killed John Lennon. He'd always liked John Lennon and he couldn't understand why anyone would want to do him.

On page four, there was a story about a teenage prostitute found strangled in the men's room at the Cloverleaf. Police said it was part of a local crime wave. All the girl's money had been taken. It meant that some greedy bastard had slipped in after him and finished her off. The cops would find his semen in her mouth and the night clerk would describe him. He wondered whether the composite drawing would look like him. Then he flipped to the classified ads and circled a job in a hardware store, mixing paint. He would see about it in the morning.

By the time he got up, however, he had changed his mind. He crossed his room and opened the closet. He imagined the rot thickening, caking dry along the sides of the pot. Behind the pot, in a white plastic bag, there was a can of shoe polish and a small old revolver. He liked the way it fitted snugly into his hand. He stepped back into the room, aiming it at the few pieces of furniture and at his own reflection in the closet door mirror. He watched himself cock the hammer with his thumb. The cylinder moved, a bullet rotated past the pin. When he pulled the trigger, the pin landed on an empty chamber.

The acid hit an hour later. It was still raining and he was standing with his hands in his coat pocket, watching people go to work. He had blackened his hands and face with shoe polish and he looked like a black man with his hair conked.

What he liked was looking at the make-up on women's faces. They too were wearing masks, and underneath he could see their real faces, the small, pinched mouths, the old age - everything they were trying to hide. Businessmen went by and he could see broken blood vessels in their cheeks. Their skin was like plastic and it began to dissolve, revealing skulls, muscles and ligament. One man had his jaw fall off and he scuttled past with a hand covering his missing chin. A squad car pulled up to the curb with two cops inside. One of them rolled down the window.

"Hey you," the cop said.

"Me?" John said, pointing at himself.

"Yeah, you."

John put his hand in his pocket. His finger curled around the gun.

"What's your name," the officer said.

"John Godfrey."

"You got ID? You got a driver's license?"

"No, sir," John lied. The picture on it showed he was white.

"What you got then?"

"I got a Social Insurance card," he said. He pulled it out of his wallet while his fingers pushed his poem deeper inside.

"All right," the cop said. "Where you live?"

"Come on, Charlie," the other officer said.

"All right," Charlie said. "But you keep moving. We come back and you're still here, you're gonna go for a ride. Understood?"

"Yes sir." The car pulled into the traffic. "Suck this, Charlie!" he shouted after it, and laughed.

The Dusseldorf restaurant, with its high-backed wooden booths, was a few blocks away on Robson Street. There were always shabby students there, and kids with parrot-red and yellow hair, a few retired German gentlemen playing chess, and young European sailors who sat in the back selling smuggled radios, cameras, watches and pens.

John slid into a booth occupied by the small bearded fellow from the Peace House and his girlfriend. He sat across the table from him and beside the girlfriend, trapping them.

"I think I'm going to kill somebody," John said. His face was wet and the shoe polish was streaked where he'd wiped it with his sleeve.

"Is that you, John?" the bearded fellow said.

John smiled, revealing the tell-tale stain where his tooth was chipped. The bearded fellow glanced at the door. He touched a knife near his plate.

"Don't do that," John said.

The bearded fellow moved his hand away. "You mean just anybody?" he asked.

John smiled again, his gums pink.

"But why, John?"

"Why not," John said.

"There must be a reason."

"Yeah, there must be."

"Well, what is it?"

John brushed the hair away from his forehead. A strand curled and fell back again. "I got to get a haircut," he mumbled.

"John, the reason?"

"I told you the reason. In my poem."

"Tell me again."

John slipped his hand into his pocket. The feel of the gun comforted him. "The fun of it," he said.

"John, that's not a reason. You can't just kill a man for the fun of it."

"Okay, you're the big writer. You tell me."

"John, I want to help you."

"Help me? You want to help me kill somebody?"

Very slowly, the bearded fellow reached across the table and let his hand fall on John's wrist. "Don't you see. Killing someone would be like interrupting a poem."

John jerked his hand free. "You're trying to trick me," he said. His other hand tightened on the gun.

"All I want is for you to control yourself."

"Bullshit, man. You're trying to trick me just like when you read your fucking poem."

The bearded fellow wet his lips. "All I did was read my poem."

"Yeah, you fucking put me to sleep man!"

Slowly, bravely, glancing at his girlfriend, the bearded fellow said, "Did you come in here to kill me, John? Is that why you came in?"

The question made John smile. "I don't know yet," he said, pulling the hammer back with his thumb. He leaned back against the booth's wooden sides, savouring the moment. "It isn't really up to me to decide. Like, maybe it's you, maybe it's me. Maybe it's the next guy. It all depends."

"On what?" the bearded fellow said. "What does it depend on, John?"

"On luck," he said and pulled the trigger.

The bearded fellow looked surprised. "What do you mean?" he said.

"I mean you're just plain fucking lucky," John said. Then he got up, left the table, and stepped out onto Robson Street.

THE MYTH OF JOEL ICKERMAN

Now that his poems are anthologized and taught to our children from coast to coast, it is easy to forget the furore his four letter words aroused when a small magazine first printed them in the summer of 1946. Condemned as obscene, assailed with vehemence by other poets in other magazines, the story was eventually picked up by the mass circulation press. A nationally syndicated columnist demanded to know why the publishers of such scurrilous filth were being supported by government grants. Public opinion was outraged and would not rest until the RCMP had impounded the entire edition. Brash, arrogant, full of passion, vitality and spleen, Chaim Avery was famous overnight.

Of course his detractors were wrong. Time has since proven this. Indeed, so completely has he changed our way of seeing things, that it is hard to imagine what all the fuss was about. His was simply a new voice, his poems bouquets of a different, more earthy odour, as noisy and unwelcome to that staid literary scene as Bacchus at a Baptist prayer meeting. His satiric poem "How shall I lay thee, let me count the ways," put the post-Romantic, daffodilian traditions of this country first to shame, then, mercifully, to an end.

That there was another, profounder, side to his nature and his poetry should have been evident even then, at least so it seems in retrospect, but no one paid attention to it. It was the audacity of what he said, namely, that sex was a pleasurable thing, which deafened his hearers' ears to all else and which caused a generation of breathless female reporters to describe his hairy chest, the boxer's thrust of his chin, and the compulsion they felt to say yes when he invariably propositioned them.

61

I must confess that, in light of this loathing and adulation, I am at a loss to explain why it was that the Jewish private school, where I was a student and Avery taught, didn't fire him. Perhaps it was the thinly disguised anti-Semitism of some of the attacks, the community forced to defend its own. Or, more likely it seems to me, it may have been that Rabbi Zuckerman, the principal who taught us Hebrew and geography, hadn't read the papers and didn't know. Certainly, it happened more than once that we were required to memorize the names of English colonies which, unnoticed by Rabbi Zuckerman, had won their independence at the end of the Second World War. And just as certainly, when Avery lectured us on the poems of John Donne, or read us parts of Rabelais or the unexpurgated plays of Shakespeare, we were careful to close the classroom door lest some of the unorthodox things he had to say might fall on Rabbi Zuckerman's ears.

If this short memoir serves no other purpose, it will at least make clear to those, in after years, who study the work of this man, that his gifts were not confined to poetry alone, for he was a dedicated and talented teacher as well. The excitement we felt waiting for his classes to start! When he entered the room with his characteristic strutting walk, his grim face would remind us of the seriousness of the business which we were about to begin. We were acolytes being initiated into a mystery and sometimes it seemed as if we were in the presence of Micah or Isaiah and that Joseph's coat of prophecy was being lowered on our shoulders. Not that Avery's classes were so high-minded that they were glum. On the contrary, like the man himself, they were filled with laughter, invective and, above all, fun. There was a way he had of widening his lids while lowering his brow which made his eyes seem even more vital than they usually did and which gave the impression that he had seen some cosmic joke at the centre of things. I remember how he'd read a line, and read it again, sucking in his breath and gesturing with his hand as if he held between his fingers the most delicious forbidden fruit and he was offering us a taste of it. And indeed there was something, if not feminine, then serpentine, about the spell he cast upon out classroom Eden.

And while there cannot have been many who were not touched in this way, his influence was especially great amongst a small coterie who sometimes accompanied him to a restaurant. How, when I was in the younger grades, I envied them! It was easy to know who they were - I mean aside from the Avery swagger of their walk and the adopted stridency of their speech - for they also refused to wear their skull caps into school. It was Joel Ickerman, the coterie's acknowledged leader, who was the first to take his off.

Poor Rabbi Zuckerman! If he'd had more hair I'm sure he would have torn it out by its roots. As it was, he threatened Joel with expulsion and Joel, to everyone's amazement, refused to back down. The school was in an uproar. There was shouting in the halls and we all tumbled out of our classes to see what was going on. I turned a corner just in time to see Joel grab the rabbi's arm and hold him in the air. Apparently, the rabbi had tried to strike him with his cane and Joel, who even then stood six feet tall, had decided to defend himself.

In the end, the rest of the coterie took their skull caps off as well and Rabbi Zuckerman was forced to choose between expelling all of them or giving in. He gave in.

It was after this episode, I believe, that Avery began to see in Joel a kindred spirit struggling to express itself. He became as solicitous as a father to the boy and it was not uncommon, after school, to see them strolling along the tree-lined esplanade, the poet, short and stocky, staring fondly at his protege. I can still see their backs disappearing from view, Joel, his head and shoulders stooped to catch the meaning of some phrase, his left arm curled around his heavy load of books the way a quarterback holds a football. Sometimes they argued volubly, shouting their conflicting interpretations of political events or poetry, Joel's brush-cut head bent, the muscles of his neck straining to reinforce his views.

Of course, Avery prevailed. His was the maturer vision. But his object was not so much to win the argument as to teach the art of argument. It was noticed that Joel, always pugnacious, now became intransigent. One no longer talked to Joel, one acquiesced. And whereas I had once been jealous of the coterie, now Joel was envied by the rest.

"Ninety-nine, point nine, nine, nine per cent of your fellow human beings," Avery said, "are trash. Vermin. Sheep. The question is, which are you? Are you one of the vast majority who seeks safety in the herd? Or are you one of those rare, inexplicable individuals, someone who rises above the common, wriggling mass and strikes out on his own?" And here Avery would stare around the room as if daring someone among us to prove himself by levitating on the spot. That Joel Ickerman belonged to the .001 elite was obvious to all of us.

At the age of sixteen, to our intense chagrin, he published his first book of poems. Looking back on them now they seem mere adolescent scribblings. But the book contained a foreword by Avery and the cover had been illustrated by Avery's wife. Even those of us who secretly believed that we had written better things were forced to admit that we could not fill a book. His output was prodigious. And, to make matters worse, he followed it up' with another, even thicker that the first, within a year.

But most galling of all was Rachel. She had long, well-shaped legs and well-developed breasts. We could see her, after school, waiting for Joel beside her bike, her cut-off shorts white and tantalizing to those of us who spent our nights groaning over photographs of naked women, especially when, with a loud halloo, Joel would rush down the steps and lift her into the air and then let her slide, slowly, down the front of him. We had no doubt she slept with him. For one thing, it was in his poems. But, more decisively, it was known that Joel had a room of his own downtown and when they left together it was obvious in which direction they were going.

Thus it was with a collective sigh of relief that we greeted the news that Joel had graduated with the school's top honours. At last there would be room for the rest of us and I, for one, had ecstatic visions of myself, listening attentively, walking the esplanade with Avery while he discussed and praised my poems. Of course we congratulated Joel, and congratulated him again when he announced that, before going on to McGill University, he would spend the summer in Paris. Paris! The Left Bank! Our heads swam with the images this conjured up for us of vermillion-mouthed whores, bidets and urinals and dirty streets and decadent cafes where poets and artists meet and argue and share their mistresses and their bottles of green absinthe. And now that he would be safely away from us, we looked forward to his return to McGill and the battles which we knew he'd wage and which we knew he'd been trained for. For we were not unaware that one of Avery's oldest enemies would be Joel's professor in his first year.

Nor were stories of his derring-do long in coming. We heard, for example, that during a particularly heated argument, Joel had ripped his textbook into shreds and had flung the pieces at this teacher's head. Berated as incompetent, an ignoramus, a eunuch, a smug, antediluvian sloth and, horror of horrors, a nattering nincompoop of a Wasp, the professor had fled the room. This time, of course, Joel was expelled but later reinstated because of his marks. Meanwhile, he brought out a new book of poems and, when the editor of the university's poetry magazine refused to print him, published an alternative anthology himself.

But to those of us who had hoped, now that Joel Ickerman was gone, that a closer association with Avery would ensue, there was nothing but disappointment. Apparently he was capable of such a relationship only once. Certainly, we tried. I, for my part, aside from the manuscript of poems I cradled in my arms, went so far as to move out from home in my final year, although I had been perfectly happy there, so desperate was I to attract his attention. I remember, in particular, one fine spring night knocking at Avery's door. His wife answered and invited me in.

"Chaim will be right with you," she smiled, leaving me in his book-lined livingroom. I believe I had a form of teenage crush on the man because I was struck, even shocked, by her use of his first name. And I recall thinking what an unfair advantage she, being a woman, had. How casually she seemed to take his fame!

I was standing, reading the titles of his books, when Avery came in and clapped me heartily on the shoulder. But when he saw my nervous, troubled look, his eyes became quite tender and full of sympathy.

"I was hoping, sir, that you would read my poems and tell me what you think." I handed him my manuscript and noticed that he looked instantly relieved.

"Of course!" he said smiling and motioning me to sit. "For a minute I thought you were going to tell me you'd gotten syphilis or married or something equally disagreeable."

He sat down breathing heavily at his own joke, put his glasses on and began to read. As I fidgeted at the edge of my chair, he flipped the flimsy pages rapidly, only pausing here and there to purse his lips or nod his head. Suddenly he peered over his glasses and looked at me.

"Would you like a drink?" he asked.

"No, sir, I'd rather take it like a man."

It took him a moment to realize I meant his criticism, but then he laughed and looked at me again.

"I gather from one of your poems that you've moved away from home."

"Yes sir, but I'm thinking of moving back. It seems I can't stand my own cooking."

This was a deviation from the path of poetic independence, one which I knew would arouse his ire and, I hoped, his interest. I was quickly disappointed.

"I'm afraid that's a decision I can't help you with," he said, going back to reading my poems. I thought he flipped through them more rapidly than before but, by then, I was impatient for him to come to the end myself.

"Not bad," he said, knocking the sheets together neatly and handing them back to me. "Not bad at all. I like some of your lines and images very much. On the whole, very promising."

He stood up and once again clapped me on the arm. Another might have taken this as a gesture of encouragement. But I knew Avery well enough by then to know that he was trying not to hurt my feelings. Perhaps he felt that he had been a bit abrupt for as I was making my way to the door, he said, "Have you got a girlfriend?"

"No, sir," I stammered, or something like that.

"Well, get one, man, get one. Preferably a blonde. A big Scandinavian. That'll take your mind off your mother's cooking. And write! Keep on writing, that's the main thing. Never mind what anyone says. You've got a genuine feel for literature, I can tell you that."

He hesitated a moment and then gave me one last clap on the arm. The door closed and behind it I could hear the creak of floorboards as he walked away.

I have no doubt that if such a blow to my self-esteem were to happen today, I would be plunged into a depression lasting for months. But such is the recuperative power of youth that, by the time the week was over, I was once again in fine spirits. In fact, I was in the middle of writing a poem when my landlady knocked on the door of my room and informed me I was wanted on the telephone. Expecting, as I did, either my father's reproach or my mother's invitation to dinner, I was surprised to hear Joel Ickerman asking if I'd like to spend the next day with him.

Of course, Avery had put him up to it. But I was flattered nonetheless and readily agreed. If Avery couldn't afford the time, thought I to myself as I typed up the poem which now would be shown to Joel, there was still much that could be learned from his star pupil.

We met, as pre-arranged, on a street corner at eleven the next morning. I was there early as in those days I didn't have a watch and I was afraid that he wouldn't wait for me. I saw him waving at me when he was still a block away, his height and large strides distinguishing him from the crowd. He shouted his customary halloo when he came up to me and then, à la Avery, he clapped me on the back as we started toward the harbour.

Oddly enough, although I can recall the route we took, the quality of the air, a newspaper swirling in an eddy of dust, I have only the vaguest idea of what we talked about. I presume we discussed the teachers he had known and I now had, what life was like at McGill, the advantages and disadvantages of living at home and alone. I remember stopping in Chinatown for some eggrolls "to go" and then walking to the end of a long, concrete pier and sitting down with our legs dangling over the edge. I remember that the sun was warm and that I was intensely happy. I read him my poem joyfully, out loud, and then watched his face and, across the water, the big ships with mysterious names while he read it to himself again. I already knew he didn't like it.

"Have an eggroll," he said.

"No thanks," I answered. "I'd rather take it like a man."

Of course, he didn't know what I meant and so he purpled more than usual while he scolded me for having written sentimental pap.

"Read Catullus!" he shouted. "Catullus is what you need. Now shut up and have an eggroll and listen to this." Whereupon he pulled Horace Gregory's marvellous translation out of his pocket - I have forgotten to mention that, no matter what the weather, Joel always wore a brown leather coat, the pockets of which were always greasy and broken and always filled with books - broke the spine of it energetically and began to read me poem after poem.

"*Otto's brains are small*," he read, "*Look at his head*. Now that's a masterpiece! Just two lines, but it's a masterpiece. Why? Because it's direct, concise, ironic, sarcastic, a distillate of pure venom!"

Of course, I recognized the phrase. It was one of Avery's favourites. But it was only much later, looking back on that day, that I realized I had been dealing, metaphorically, with a hologram, a three-dimensional projection without a substance of its own, a myth. Even the gestures Joel made, the way he plucked the air and sucked in his breath, reminded me of Avery and his, by now, familiar fruit. But at the time the impression he made was one of overwhelming strength, of vitality I could share but was no match for. And frankly, when he left me at the end of that long day, I skipped my supper and went to bed.

Joel lived in a basement apartment with an entrance of its own, in the weeks that followed our first meeting, I became a frequent visitor. For some reason, perhaps precisely because I was unsure of my welcome, I had developed the habit of knocking quickly and then walking in on him. Usually I would find Joel reading a book or fixing himself something to eat and the small start I would give him was good for a laugh. But on this occasion, having knocked and abruptly stepped in, my entrance was greeted with a high-pitched shriek and a tremendous flurry of sheets. Before I could move or apologize, Joel had jumped out of bed and was barring my way. He was shouting at me, no doubt telling me to get out of the room, but my attention was not on what he said. Between the sheets I had caught a glimpse of Rachel's pink thigh and now, in front of me, naked and angry, stood Joel in all his masculine glory. I myself had not yet had sex and the sight of Joel, still wet with it, rendered me incapable of observing anything else, including the elementary rules of decorum. It was only after I had been turned by the shoulders and marched out the door that I realized what a fool I had made of myself.

I was too embarrassed to apologize and the phone call I hoped for, inviting me over, never came. At McGill, the next year, I sometimes caught sight of him rushing to class, and sometimes we bumped into each other with loud halloos and walked a little way, but on the whole I preferred to avoid him.

As the years passed he put on weight and his manner, which formerly I had admired for its vitality and elan, now struck me as laboured and self-consciously insincere. Perhaps someone, perhaps Rachel, had told him that he was in danger of becoming a parody of Avery. I don't know. I do know that an inordinate amount of time had gone by without any of Joel's poems appearing, even in the little magazines. And when I ran into him at the gates to the campus one day, he informed me that he was switching to political science.

"But why, Joel?" I asked.

"Because I don't want to end up like some academic eunuch lisping the lines of Blake. If I've got to teach to earn a living I'd rather teach political science."

"Seems reasonable enough," I said. "How's Avery?"

"Great! Just great. He read me his latest poems. Magnificent things. We argue about politics all the time."

We parted and I walked away feeling disheartened and yet triumphant at the same time.

Meanwhile, great changes had been occurring in our cultural milieu. The beatnik hipster type had spread until practically anyone under thirty called himself a hippie. The watchwords now were 'be cool' and 'be laid back' and suddenly Joel's strident manner was as outmoded as his brush-cut head. The movement even reached as far as Israel where I was studying for my M.A. at the University of Jerusalem and where, along with most of my generation, I experimented with grass and hashish.

Still, I was surprised to discover upon my return that Joel had been experimenting with them as well. I had met him in the street and, frankly astonished at the roll of fat beneath his chin, I said, "I see you've put on a little weight."

He laughed good-naturedly, in a self-deprecating way that I'd never seen in him before, and invited me back to his apartment. He still lived in the same place and, on the way, he gave me news of our mutual acquaintances and, inevitably, of Avery.

"Have you read his latest book?" he asked.

"Yes," I said as noncommittally as I could. But then, sensing that my views, for once, would not be met with a tirade, I added, "I'm afraid I found it somewhat repetitive."

Joel was silent for a moment, as if weighing what he wanted to say. "He's going through a rough time of it. His wife left him and, I guess you know, Rabbi Zuckerman finally fired him."

"No, I didn't. When did this happen?"

"A few months ago. Somebody translated one of his poems into Hebrew and Zuckerman read it."

"You're kidding!" I said. "They don't even have words for that sort of thing in Hebrew."

"I am kidding," Joel laughed. "I don't know how Zuckerman found out."

It was the first time I'd ever heard Joel crack a joke. I looked at him more closely now and realized that his brush-cut had grown. It reminded me oddly of the pockets of his coat. Greasy and broken, it fell over his forehead, giving him a gentler, almost befuddled, look. I was wondering what might have caused this change when he opened the door to his room and I understood. Never tidy, the place now was a shambles. Records, books, magazines and newspaper clippings, assorted bits of clothing, dirty plates and cutlery were strewn across the basement floor. The bed was unmade and various odds and ends littered the only chair. But most significant was the ashtray near the bed. In it I recognized a hash pipe and the butts of several marijuana cigarettes.

"You smoke?" I asked in that conspiratorial tone of voice which indicated I didn't mean tobacco.

He nodded his head and asked me if I wanted some.

"Far out!" I said using one of those watchwords which I detested but which I sometimes threw in for ironic effect.

"As far as I can get." Another joke! And then, clearing a place for me on the chair, he said, "But he'll be all right. Several universities have offered him a post."

"Who? Oh, you mean Avery." Joel by this time was lighting the pipe and sucking in the air with gusto. Some cruel streak in me made me say, "Aren't you afraid he'll turn into an academic eunuch?"

Joel, caught off-guard, coughed and lost his toke. He handed me the pipe while he replied.

"No. He'll be all right. He knows the score. He won't fall for their crap."

"What about you?" I asked, handing him back the pipe. "You must be a professor by now."

"I give a seminar once a week." He sucked in the smoke and his face reddened while he held his breath. When he spoke again it was slowly and little puffs of smoke, expelled from his lungs, punctuated his remarks. "But I'm going to drop it as soon as I can. It ties me down. Do you realize," he said, indicating the room, "that I've been living in this place for ten years? One of these days I'm going to fly the coop. I haven't been anywhere since that summer I took off to Paris."

"Speaking of Paris," I said, taking my turn on the pipe, "I stopped over there on my way back from Jerusalem. What did you think of it?"

"Paris? Dead. Completely dead. I remember, during the flight, looking at the clouds and imagining a city there. That's what Paris should have been like. A city of the imagination! Instead, I scuttled like a dung-beetle from one cafe to another and all I found were drunk tourists like myself."

He paused and took another toke. A quiet settled on us. The pipe passed back and forth. When he spoke again it was a softer, more reflective voice.

"The truth is, I was too young, too precocious, too impetuous. I wasn't ready for Paris but I wanted to spread my wings. I wanted to go too far, too fast. That has always been my downfall."

"Joel," I said firmly, knocking the contents of the pipe into the ashtray and deliberately putting it out, "I think you're getting a little too high."

"No, I'm not. I'm getting depressed."

I spent the better part of the next hour trying to jolly him out of it, waiting for the effects of the hash to wear off. I asked him where he'd like to travel and he said he thought Tibet. I told him about the mysterious air in the mountains of Jerusalem and he said he'd like to go there too. He had plenty of money, he said, his father was rich. By the time I left we had both agreed that the future was bright and full of prospects. But when I awoke the next morning, I felt a vague presentiment and made a mental note to check on Joel again that afternoon.

I was relieved, when he opened the door, to see that he looked better that he had the previous evening. His brush-cut was combed and again stood straight up and he had tidied up his room.

"I was a little worried about you last night," I said. "I think you'd better lay off the hash for a while."

"Yes, I will," he said, clapping me on the arm as if to indicate that he was in perfect health. "You know, a funny thing happened after you left. I went upstairs to make a phone call - you know the phone is in the hall - and suddenly I couldn't move. I had the receiver against my ear but I couldn't lift my finger to dial the number!"

"Far out," I said. "How long did it last?"

"I don't know. At least an hour. And the worst thing was, I could hear the dial tone but I couldn't put the receiver down. You have no idea how painful it is to listen to a dial tone for a solid hour."

Of course, I thought this was merely an amusing hash after-effect and we both laughed at the absurdity of it. It wasn't until much later that evening, when Rachel called on me at my parent's home, that I learned how serious the incident had really been.

"Is Joel here?" she demanded as soon as I came to the door. Her eyes were accusing and angry.

"No. Why? What's the matter?"

"Where is he then?"

"How should I know!" I was getting angry myself. "I haven't seen him since this afternoon."

"So you saw him this afternoon. Did you smoke dope with him?"

"Sh! Not so loud. My parents might hear. No, not this afternoon. We did some last night. Why? For heaven's sake, Rachel, will you tell me what's happened?"

"For your information, Joel was taken to the Institute last night. His landlady heard him start to make a phone call but he didn't say anything. She found him in the hall, catatonic, just standing there. After an hour she called the police. They've diagnosed him as some sort of schizophrenic."

"Oh, Rachel, they call everyone schizophrenic. I tell you I saw him just this afternoon. He was perfectly normal."

"Sure he was. That's the problem. All of a sudden, this morning, he snapped out of it. They couldn't hold him against his will and he said he wanted to get some of his things. He was supposed to voluntarily commit himself this evening but he hasn't shown up."

In the end they found him somewhere in the city, frozen immobile at a stoplight.

I learned afterwards that, during my absence in Israel, Joel had finally brought out a book of poems. Actually, it was only one poem, an epic flight of fancy which the critics claimed was an imitation of Avery and quickly shot down in flames. A few weeks later, according to Rachel, he was caught trying to jump off a bridge. It required all of Avery's considerable influence to keep the news out of the papers.

It would be several years before I saw Joel again and then it was only to catch a glimpse. I was on vacation from my teaching duties at Cornell and visiting my parents as usual. Feeling the tug of nostalgia, I had decided to take a walk past the haunts of my student days. In fact, I was thinking about Joel when, still quite a distance away, I saw him going into a restaurant. I was filled with excitement and hurried to catch up with him.

"Halloo, Joel!" I said as I sat down at his table and waited for him to recognize me. I'm not sure that he did. But instead of greeting me, his face took on a haunted look and he immediately stood up. There was a bowl of soup on the table in front of him and he upset it as he rushed away, leaving me to pay the bill.

————

Here, I suppose, my story would have ended were it not for the fact that a student of mine, at Cornell, wanted to do her doctorate on Avery. She was intrigued by the Apollonian aspects of his poetry and this was such an innovative idea, at least to me who had always thought of him as Dionysian, that I decided to reread his poems.

Of course, she was right. There was a more formal, symbolic side to his work which all of us, dazzled by his sexual pyrotechnics, had ignored. Rereading his books I realized that Avery had been watching the antics of his fellow man as if from a very great height, as if his very art depended upon charting a middle course between the Charybdis of emotion and the Scylla of dispassionate intellect.

But there was also something in his later poems which I found quite disturbing, a tone of self-reproach, as if the immortal poet within were mocking the failures of the man. Certainly, his early preoccupation with sex was now counterbalanced by an awareness of death and I wondered whether the plunge of Joel Ickerman into insanity, and his attempt at suicide, had been a factor in all of this. For there was no denying that Joel had been like a son to the man and that Avery, in teaching him the secrets of his craft, had set the boy's mind on fire with an idea which eventually consumed him. It was inevitable that he should feel responsible and yet, from all accounts, Avery never visited him, had even become, so it was said, something of a recluse.

I had decided to approach Avery on my student's behalf and, the next time I visited my parents, I called on him as well. He lived, it turned out, alone in a high-rise apartment building in a conventional part of town. It was a beautiful day, one of the first fine days of summer, and when he opened the door the sunlight from his windows lit the back of his head and silvered his graying hair.

"Good to see you!" he cried, clapping me on the back of the arm, a little tentatively I thought, as if testing to see whether he still had the right to do so. "My god, how long has it been? Fifteen years?"

"At least! You're looking well."

"Thank you. Thank you. You're not looking so bad yourself. Getting a little bald I see."

"I'm afraid I am," I said, instinctively touching the offending spot as he motioned me to a chair. He was obviously unused to his duties as host and remained hovering above me while we spoke.

"Would you care for a drink?"

"Thank you. That would be very nice."

"What would you like?" he asked nervously.

I told him scotch on the rocks and he complimented me on my good taste. "That's what I drink myself," he said and hurried off to the kitchen to get the ice.

His absence gave me a chance to survey the room. It was sparsely furnished, painted white and, for a man living alone, surprisingly clean and neat. The walls were bare, almost opaline in the light, and when he came back in I asked him what had happened to all his books.

"Oh, my wife took a great many," he said matter of factly, setting down our drinks. "And I gave some to friends." He smiled almost apologetically and finally sat down. "So what brings you here? You said something about a student's thesis on the phone."

I was in the middle of explaining her proposal, the importance of it and the plan of attack, when he interrupted me to ask whether I was still in touch with any of his former students. I gave him what news I could. Most were professional men, lawyers, doctors, college profs like myself. A few had gone into their fathers' businesses and were doing very well.

"And you?"

I shrugged. "Life has its ups and downs."

"Are you married?"

"Yes," I laughed. "And it's your fault."

"My fault? What do you mean?"

"Well, you told me to get myself a big Scandinavian blonde and that's what I did."

"Oh, I see. But surely I didn't tell you to marry her!"

"No, you didn't. But just her being Scandinavian was bad enough. If I'd lived in sin with her as well, my parents would have killed themselves."

Perhaps it was the idea of suicide. I don't know. But some train of thought led Avery, quite unexpectedly, to ask it I'd heard from Joel.

"No," I said, feeling I had better tread delicately. "I understand he's still in the Institute."

"I suppose you know he tried to commit suicide."

"Yes. More that once, I'm told."

"Do you know why?"

"Well, not really, no. But I - I always felt he was living a sort of myth, if you know what I mean. I thought he was imitating you to an unhealthy degree."

"In other words you think I was a bad influence on him."

"I didn't say that."

"Well, I did! That's what everybody's been thinking for years!"

I think the vehemence with which he said these words surprised even himself. He swallowed the rest of his drink and then sat for a moment staring at the bottom of his empty glass. When he spoke again, it was with the cunning passion of a man trying to defend his integrity.

"Of course I blamed myself! After Joel cracked up I had to ask myself whether he'd really had the makings of a poet, or had I, in my enthusiasm, taken a sensitive, but ordinary kid and ruined his life for him. And was it just enthusiasm? Or were my motives rooted in the vanity and egotism of wanting a disciple? And another thought, much more horrible: How was it possible for a man who's been a poet for thirty or forty years to still be so blind! So I couldn't see Joel after that. I imagined it would only have made him worse. And, besides, what did I have to say to him if poetry had failed even me?

"That, an any rate, is how my thinking went. Then, a couple of months ago, I got a call from his doctor in the hospital. He told me that Joel had just been rescued from another suicide attempt and was asking for me to come down and see him. Well, I won't go into the details of what he looked like or what else we said, but after a while I couldn't contain myself any more. 'Joel,' I said. 'Why do you keep doing this to yourself?' And do you know what he said? He told me in one word. And as soon as he said that one word you can't imagine the relief I felt. Because I knew it was true. It all made sense. And do you know what that one word was? Can you guess what's been bothering that stupid, juvenile brain all this time?" It was a rhetorical question - Avery's favourite kind - but his pause was not so much for effect as to control his gathering rage. "Impotency!" he said. "He's been impotent for years!" Again he paused, waiting for the significance of this information to sink in. "Don't you see? That's why he became such a caricature of me, such a ridiculous, pompous, strident ass! He was a phoney. His poetry was phoney. It was all a compensation for the fact that he couldn't get it up. As simple as that!

"And then I thought of how I'd blamed myself. Doubted myself. And the hours I'd spent pleading with him, telling him not to be depressed, telling him to try again, to go on writing - wasted! All that time and energy, wasted! I tell you, I was so angry that if he hadn't been half-dead already I would've strangled him!"

The grisly joke exploded Avery's temper and gave me a chance to ask about something that had begun to puzzle me.

"But when did this problem begin?" I said.

"Years ago when he was just a kid. That time he flew to Paris. He told me the whole story. Some Parisian whore made him so nervous he couldn't perform and the bitch made fun of him. It could have happened to anyone. But to a sensitive kid like Joel, because he *was* sensitive, because he *was* a poet, it was shattering. But would he tell me about it? Would he let me help him? It would have been the easiest thing to tell him it was normal, or get a doctor for him or some understanding woman."

"What about Rachel?" I asked. "Surely she helped him."

"Rachel! Don't talk to me about Rachel! She's the one who made him worse. Here he comes back from Paris, desperately in need of her love, needing above all her reassurance, and she never let him sleep with her. She refused! He told me all about it."

I was too stunned, and too polite, to object. It was obvious that Joel's explanation was very important to Avery and I did not feel it was my place to tell him what I knew. But I remembered Joel standing naked in front of me and Rachel's long legs between the sheets. No, whatever else, impotence was not the reason and I wondered whether Joel had invented it, not for his own sake, but for Avery. It was a chilling thought. For a moment it occurred to me that Joel might not be insane at all. Or, if insane, that perhaps, in the traumatic aftermath of his attempted suicide, he had had a period of sudden lucidity and had thought of a way to bless his teacher and all his works with an act of mercy and great forgiveness.

But I said nothing and we went on to discuss my student's thesis.

CURRICULUM VITAE

Contrast

>   *I walk a canvas road*
>   *I breathe a painted cloud*

with

>   *I walk the streets at night*
>   *Knife in hand and aimed at nothing*

and you'll see what I mean. The first rhythm merely repeats itself.
The second uncoils like a spring. The first is vacuous and artsy-
fartsy. The second is full of menace. The first was published in a
precious, leather-bound volume several years ago. The second
appeared in a recent issue of *Preview Review.* Both were by the
same author. Suddenly, inexplicably, Malcolm Ravitch had begun
writing real poetry.

I read further:

>   *If a women is a donkey*
>   *Then my cock a carrot is*
>   *By means of it I've journeyed*
>   *The deepest inner distances*
>
>   *Oh, eager beasts of burden*
>   *On your slender backs I've ridden*
>   *To all the far off corners*
>   *Of my bed.*

I was envious and chagrined, even conscience-struck. Not,
mind you, because I was envious - that, when an older poet reads
good work by a younger, is in the normal course of things - but

because, not six months earlier, I had descended from the heights of Mount Parnassus and, in the very same pages of *Preview Review*, lambasted Malcolm for his complacency and sterility. I regarded him as the worst sort of scheming academic hack, the sort who makes a comfortable living as a professor of English Literature and who then writes poetry bemoaning his own aesthetic aridity, the sort who can always count on a Canada Council grant or who, after years of contributing nothing to the country's culture except a pervasive mood of impotence and despair, nevertheless runs away with the Governor-General's Award.

From what I could gather, Malcolm's career had begun in the early seventies when his *alma mater* (Yale) published his first book of poems. Perhaps there had been a surplus of funds, perhaps he had politicked, perhaps some academic actually liked his adolescent maunderings - I don't know - but, because he had been published by Yale, the book was respectfully reviewed. "Promising," said the *New York Times.* "A new talent," said *Preview Review.* (And why not? Who, in this day and age when no one can tell the difference between a work of art and a flush toilet, wants to take upon himself the awesome responsibility of destroying a young man's career?)

But, because he had been respectfully reviewed, and because he had been published by Yale, his next book was taken by Random House; Jonathan Cape, in England, wanted him too. And because he had been published by Jonathan Cape and Random, again he was respectfully reviewed.

There was only one catch: his books didn't sell. After a few more tries, his manuscripts were refused.

That's when Malcolm moved to Canada.

His credentials impeccable, his poetry - innocuous, anaemic and trivial - frequently appearing, Malcolm Ravitch burst upon the Canadian scene and quickly made himself indispensable. He wrote learned appreciations of other poets' work. He gave lectures at symposia and attended conferences. If you wanted a scholarship or a grant, his recommendation was decisive. By the time I met him, after years of avoiding him, he had become a cultural arbiter. He had a posh house in a posh part of town. He was a full professor married to a rather plain and petulant-looking wife. He was paunchy, mid-forty, self-satisfied. He was also self-effacing - something I despised. I can't stand small, balding but ambitious men who say flattering things and who contrive, when you meet them, to appear gracious, hospitable and shy. Looking back on that meeting now, I believe his bashfulness was due to my reputation and his genuine regard for my work. But at the time he reminded me of small dogs I've observed who roll over on their backs and pee. I hated Malcom Ravitch and everything he stood for and it was shortly after this that I wrote my diatribe.

And then, out of the blue, these marvellous poems - poems which could only have been written by someone deeply moved. But by what? What could make this middle-aged professor walk the streets with a knife? What could possibly blind an opportunist like Malcolm Ravitch to the fact that, in this era of rampant feminism and politically correct speech, he had likened a women to a donkey?

Whatever it was, I had obviously misjudged: There were depths to the man of which I had had no inkling. I was determined to apologize - in fact, I accepted an invitation to a poetry conference in Moncton, New Brunswick, simply because I knew he was going to be there - but before I could do so I learned along the grape-vine that Gregory James, a handsome young poet and Malcolm's best friend, was having an affair with Malcolm's wife. As usual, everyone seemed to know about this except Malcolm. The scuttle-butt at the poetry conference concerned very little else. I felt sorry for him and, since I knew I had done him a wrong, I decided to make it up to him by telling him myself.

I recall that the first evening of the conference was almost over before I spotted him on the other side of the room. Drinks had been served and we were all standing around in little groups talking about the lecture on Synthetic Poetry we had just heard. I went up to him and drew him aside.

"Malcolm," I said. "I feel I owe you an apology. I liked those poems in *Preview Review* very much."

It was an uncomfortable position for both of us. I didn't want to appear condescending and yet here I was, the older poet who had just attacked him in public, privately praising his poems. He, on the other hand, while undoubtedly gratified, could only accept my praise if he swallowed his pride.

Finally he said, "Will you print a retraction?"

I wasn't prepared for that. But I drew myself up and answered, "Of course. If you insist."

He looked at me with surprise. "That's truly magnanimous. Unfortunately, I agreed with everything you said."

"Nonsense. It's clear to me now that you are anything but sterile. I can tell you are suffering some torment - it's in those poems - some discontent..."

I let the sentence hang in the air, hoping he would tell me - as I now suspected - that the problem was his wife's infidelity. Instead, he became agitated and - was it my imagination? - furtive.

"Malcolm," I said gently. "Everyone knows."

This time there was no surprise. "Knows what?" he said. But he said it mechanically, his mind buying time to think. And then he gave up. There was no use pretending. He knew that I knew his secret. He had known about his wife all along.

He took me by the arm and led me down a stairwell off the main auditorium. He stood staring at me and then he took his glasses off and I could see that, without them, his eyes were liquid and unfocused. He sat down on a stair and I sat down beside him. He put his hands between his knees.

"What was your motive?" he asked after a while.

"What do you mean?"

"I mean, why did you want to tell me? What for?"

"I thought I'd be doing you a favour," I said. "It only occurred to me at the last moment that you already knew."

"But why? Why do me any favours?"

"I had misjudged you. Not just your poems, but you. I owed you something."

"And that's it?"

"More or less."

"*More or less.* Tell me, weren't you just a little bit curious?"

I thought about this. "Among other things."

"But you were curious, right? Aside from your sympathy and doing me favours and everything else, a piece of you was just plain itching to see how I'd take it, right?"

"A piece of me, yes."

"So, actually, you must have been disappointed. I already knew, surprise, surprise! Right?"

"A piece of me, perhaps. But that wasn't my motive. Not in this case. It could have been, but not in this case. I happen to be writing about something else."

He put his glasses back on and looked at me closely, as if he were seeing me for the first time.

"So you do it too," he said.

"Of course."

"*Of course, of course!* But what if I told you that I connived - that I willed it to happen? That I deliberately *didn't* put an end to the whole revolting thing because I found it absolutely fascinating! What then?"

"It wouldn't surprise me. Look, nobody said poets were --"

But he had lifted his hand and turned his head away queerly, not wanting to hear.

"I find the whole thing disgusting," he said. He made a small fist and turned back to me. "I should have boxed Gregory in the ear."

"Well, why didn't you?"

"Because..." And here Malcom's face flushed with anger and self-loathing. "I was writing poem after poem. Great poems. Poems that, for the first time in my life - well, you said it yourself. I mean, how I could have hit the sonofabitch with a clear conscience when what I felt was - grateful! Even now, now that you've told me, now that I'm going to have to do something about it, do you want to know the first thing that flashed through my mind - what's really bothering me? I'm worried about what I'm going to write about next!"

I was filled, as so often happens, with both sympathy and aversion. I patted his shoulder and he calmed down. "I'm afraid that's something I can't help you with," I said, hoping for a laugh. He forced a smile and then we went back up the stairs and rejoined the others.

It wasn't until a few months had gone by that I decided to write this down. I had just read some of Gregory James' poems in the most recent issue of *Preview Review*. They were urgent and anguished and very, very good.

MY YARMULKA

Things came to a head back in 1966, before the Arab-Israeli war broke out, back in the days when I still wore my yarmulka - mostly to provoke my parents, I think, because my father, although Jewish, was an atheist and my mother, although Scottish, was converted. This she had done when I was one year old - in fact, my parents had only married when I was one year old - so I was a *mamser* on top of everything else. Not a bastard, mind you, but a *mamser*, a Jewish bastard - which was a consolation.

I remember, at the age of four or five, when we had just moved to the suburbs, sitting in a circle in a field with my new-found friends. Anthony Kazha was Hungarian, he said. Tony Tiber was German. Leo Doucette was French-Canadian. Ronnie Kingsley was Anglo-Irish and Jimmy McWilliam was just plain Irish. And I? I didn't know. I remember running home. My father was upstairs shaving.

"Daddy," I said, "Anthony Kazha is Hungarian and Tony Tiber is German. What about me? What am I?"

The razor cut a swath through the pure white lather underneath his chin. His free hand followed the razor carefully palpating the skin to see if it was smooth because it was a tricky spot and he had a permanent scar there from nicking it so often. I was fascinated watching him and had almost forgotten my question.

He drew himself up proudly, like a father should in front of his son, in front of a mirror, and said, "You're Jewish, my boy. You belong to the oldest people on the earth."

"Oh, goody," I said and rushed down the stairs and out of the house.

I came back in with my lip bleeding and sand in my hair. I was crying with rage and frustration. I had been beating Jimmy McWilliam, but then Anthony Kazha had grabbed me from behind and Tony Tiber had sat on me and twisted my arm up my back. I remember my mother, again as a consolation, taking me to see a Walt Disney film about nature. I remember a sidewinder moving across the desert floor and striking a small, terrified mouse. It unhinged its jaws and swallowed and I was so intent upon watching this that I stopped crying for myself.

But why was I Jewish and not Scottish? My mother, who had converted, was certainly not Jewish - at least not to my father. To her own father - who had disowned her - she certainly was. But to my father, whenever they had an argument, you could practically hear him thinking: *Why did I marry such a pig-headed philistine? They're hopeless!* Out loud he complained bitterly about her lack of sense of humour. Out loud he said, "So I look at other women, so what? I'm sorry, but I'm not your father and I'm not your brother. I'm not some Calvinist Presbyterian."

Dour - how he loved to use that word, like a cudgel thudding against her thick, Scottish skull.

"And do me a favour," he ranted. "Don't talk to me about good manners. My people were kings in Egypt when the Scots and the Picts were still throwing stones at each other."

To me he said, "Did you know Paul Newman was Jewish?"

And not only Paul Newman. Yasha Heifitz and Yehudi Menuhin. El Greco, Modigliani, Franz Kafka. They were all Jewish.

"You want economics? Karl Marx. You want philosophy? Spinoza. Psychology? Freud. Even Christianity, for God's sake - Jesus Christ was Jewish! - No wonder they hate us. Everywhere they look, there's a goddam Jew."

But by what criteria? Spinoza had been kicked out of the Jewish community. Marx was an atheist who wrote anti-Semitic diatribes. Paul Newman was only one-quarter Jewish. Was it just because they were great that he wanted to claim them, or was there really such a thing as Jewish blood? Could it be that Hitler had been right when he said that regardless of the language you spoke or your religion, regardless of how valiantly you had fought for the Germans during the First World War, if one of your grandparents was Jewish *you* were Jewish? Of course, my father didn't think Jews should be sent to the ovens, but had he, unwittingly, accepted the Nazi definition?

But, if so, if it were merely the blood, then, why, when it suited him, was I sometimes not Jewish? Because there was no doubt in my mind that sometimes I was not. I had never worn phylacteries, would not have known what to do with them. He had to tell me what a talith was. (It was a prayer shawl.) I had never been bar-mitzvahed. I HAD NEVER BEEN BAR-MITZVAHED! Why not? Because he didn't believe in it? Or because, really, deep down, secretly, some atavistic part of him felt it would have been a sacrilege! I don't know. I never asked him. I only know the delight he got in telling a joke and then cracking the punch line in Yiddish - a language he knew I didn't know. Then he'd look at me with the look he gave my mother and I could feel my skull thickening. *Hopeless goyishe kop*, he was thinking. Out loud he said, "I'm sorry. You don't understand, I forgot. Too bad, because it loses in translation."

No, my father's vision was Manichean: If it was good, if he approved of it, if it furthered civilization, it was Jewish; if it was bad, if it was selfish or brutish or stupid, it was pagan, philistine, goyish, Wasp. In other words, Shakespeare was Jewish but Hitler, even if it were true that his grandfather was Jewish, would still have been German.

I remember him patiently explaining the burden - I use that word advisedly - the burden of Matthew Arnold's essay on the difference between the Hebrew and the Hellene. Western civilization, my father told me, was the product of the irreconcilable tension between them. "The ideal man of the Renaissance pursued greatness above all other things. But the Reformation went back to the ideal of goodness. Goodness is Jewish, greatness is pagan. Together, in one civilization, they make a contradiction. Do you know why?"

I shook my head.

"Because the highest virtue for the pagan was pride whereas, for the Jew, pride was the sin of Satan."

It was an interesting dialectic and it left my father's black eyebrows dancing on his forehead. There was only one problem: If the tension was irreconcilable, if it actually involved a contradiction, then where did I - half-Jew and half-Scotsman - fit in?

I think it was shortly after this conversation that I began wearing my yarmulka. It seemed an emblem of the sort of protection you need if your skull is thin.

"How can you wear such a thing?"

"Leave him alone," my mother said, defending me.

"But he doesn't even go to *shul*!"

"He's searching for his roots."

"So let him wear a kilt."

Later, when I could afford it, I bought a length of tartan cloth and had it made into a vest. There were jokes from my friends, but I parried them by saying that, as a Scottish Jew, I not only knew how to make money but how to save it too.

Oddly enough, the only anti-Semitism I ever experienced happened the one time I took my yarmulka off. I was going to university then, flying towards my first summer job in a lumber camp in northern B.C. There was only one other passenger and after I smiled at him nervously, he said, "A word of advice, kid. If you wear that thing in the lumber camp you'll get your head bashed in."

"Thanks," I said, and my hand flew to my yarmulka and snatched it off.

A few days later I was sitting down to dinner and - I should explain that lumberjacks have a rigid sense of cookhouse etiquette: Men who swear torrentially, magnificently, all day long refuse to utter so much as 'damn' while eating. You eat communally, by the way, with food served in the middle of the table and eight men down each side. Everyone says 'excuse me' and 'please' and no one serves himself potatoes or peas without first offering them to his neighbour. Sitting across from me was a huge, bull-necked Yugoslav, a man with shoulders so wide he had to twist sideways to get in the cookhouse door. Imagine my horror when he glowered at me and said, in his thick accented voice: "Hey, joo, pass da butter."

My first thought was, *that guy on the plane has told everyone!*

My second thought was - panic. I had been called a Jew to my face. If I didn't defend myself immediately, I'd be the butt of anti-Semitic jokes for the rest of the summer. My legs felt weak. My heart was pounding like the wheels of a freight train heading towards a concentration camp.

"What'd you say!" I snarled furiously. So this was it. He was going to take me outside and squeeze the life out of me against his massive chest.

And then, unbelievably, his face went red and his eyes bulged with fear and apology. "Hey, joo," he stammered, "pass da butter, *please.*"

"Hey, *you,*" he had meant, not "Hey, Jew."

My honour was saved and no one knew.

"That's better," I said sternly, and handed him the butter.

I had started wearing it again - my yarmulka, that is - by the time I met Erik Sorenson at the YMCA. This was in Montreal in 1966 and I had finally finished my B.A. I had taken a part-time job in a bookstore and I lived in a small room studying Hebrew and reading philosophy most of the day. My body was terribly out of shape.

It was a kind of prejudice, I suppose - I mean, not joining the YMHA. I imagined it filled with blue-veined old men wearing bathing caps, clutching at their hearts and saying "*Oy vey!*" after every exertion. No, if you wanted real exercise, the only place was the YMCA. I delighted in the smell of Christian sweat, the bang of weights being thrown on the floor, the sight of the powerful Negroes and muscled, fair-haired men standing naked and unashamed in the locker-rooms and around the pool. It was the pagan ideal, only Christianized - "Judaized," my father would say - that is, walled in and driven underground. The whole complex was an underground maze: corridors which led off to mysterious rooms - saunas and gymnasia and homosexual meeting places - and it was easy to lose your way. In fact, it was only because I had taken a wrong turn that I discovered Erik Sorenson's private school.

The door was open and I could hear a tremendous thumping coming from within. I stood in the doorway and looked inside. A young man with straight black hair was whirling in front of a canvas sand-filled bag. As he turned, his legs shot out behind him and his arms flashed from his sides and every blow that landed sent the heavy canvas bag rattling against the chains that suspended it from the ceiling.

"Too high! You're aiming too high!" A man with honey-coloured curly hair and intense blue eyes had jumped up from among several others who were sitting cross-legged on the far side of the room. He strode across the floor quickly, pulling at his beard. The young man with the black hair stopped whirling instantly. He bowed and said, "I'm sorry, *sensei.*" He stood erect.

"I don't care if you're sorry. Next time aim for the spleen." And with that he plunged two straight fingers into the young man's abdomen. "Here!" he said. The young man doubled over and began to cough. The man with the beard turned away in disgust. Then, seeing me, he said, "You, in the doorway, if you want to watch, take your shoes off and sit against the wall. Don't interrupt the class."

For the next hour I sat there impassively. I sensed that I was being watched, tested, that if I sat without moving he would talk to me. But, if I got up and left, he would never let me back in.

Although it was painful and he hadn't asked me to, I sat cross-legged like the others. I wanted to impress him with my willingness.

As I expected, when the class was finished he came over and sat down in front of me. He was absolutely humourless, I discovered, and spoke pompously.

"My name is Erik Sorenson," he said. "If you wish to be in this class, you must call me *sensei* which is a Japanese word meaning teacher, master."

So I was being admitted! Out loud I said, "Thank you, *sensei*. But what is it? Karate?"

"Karate is completely different. What I teach is unique. It is called Shao-lin."

"Shao-lin," I repeated. "Is it Chinese?"

"It is named after a Chinese monastery. But it is far more ancient. It was known to the warriors of the ancient Middle East."

For some reason, I felt my hair standing on end. "Who?" I asked. "The Babylonians?"

"I have already told you to much. I will tell you the secrets of Shao-lin when you have proved yourself worthy." Then, glancing up at my yarmulka, he said, "Are you Jewish?"

"Yes," I said. "And you?"

He seemed annoyed that I might ask him the same thing. "I am Danish," he said and looked at me significantly. However, I didn't understand his look and went on to ask him about the times and his fee. (Classes were two hours long, five days a week. He did not charge any money.) He made his living as a paramedic, he said, because it was important to know how to heal as well as how to destroy.

Over the next few weeks I got my body into shape. I did sit-ups and push-ups and lifted weights and got to the point where, if I bent from the waist with my knees straight, I could touch the floor with the palms of my hands. Once, out of curiosity, I visited a Karate class. Sorenson was right, Shao-lin was unique. In Karate, the students stood rigid and endeavoured to deliver ponderous blows, whereas we had been taught to dance on our toes and already I had learned a kind of side-kick and two or three side-arm techniques which did not seem to be in the Karate repertoire at all.

"You must learn to punch the same way you throw a ball," Sorenson said. "You stay loose until the last second, then pivot your hip and snap your shoulder. That's it! That's it!" (My wrist buckled painfully against the bag.) "No! Straighten your arm. Align your bones. Aim two or three inches beyond your target. If you're going for somebody's belly, imagine you're going all the way through until your fist is around his spinal column."

And the power he had! I remember one lesson when Jim, the black-haired student I had first seen, was again whirling in front of the bag.

"You're always showing off!" Sorenson shouted, pushing him aside. "Anyone can kick hard. The point is to kick accurately." And then Sorenson's foot lashed out at the bag and there was a sound of ripping canvas and sand poured out of the hole. Sorenson was furious at himself for having lost control. "That's it!" he said. "I don't want to see you in this class again."

"But, *sensei*," Jim pleaded.

"You heard me. Get out!"

Afterwards, Sorenson came up to me and fumed, "Young punks! All they want to do is show off. They're not interested in the discipline, the meaning."

So I was being complimented. It was just a matter of time, then, before I learned the secrets of Shao-lin.

After class one evening, about a month and a half-later, Sorenson turned to me and said, "Why do you wear a tartan vest?"

I was surprised at this because I only wore it in the mornings when I went to work. It disturbed me to think that he had been spying.

"How do you know that?" I said.

"Answer my question."

"Because my mother is Scottish."

"You said you were Jewish."

"She converted."

"That's very interesting," he said, looking at me calmly.

"Why?" I asked impertinently.

"Because I think it means you are ready."

It was the first time he had invited me to his house - a basement apartment, with an entrance of its own. I was so filled with excitement that I barely noticed the odd melange of religious symbolism - crucifixes, yin and yang, the signs of the zodiac - which he had hung on its walls. He led me into a small kitchen and made me a cup of tea. He pointed to the far side of a wooden table and I sat there, feeling a little trapped, while he stood between me and the door pulling at his beard and thinking about what he intended to say.

"The reason your being Jewish and Scottish interests me," he began, sitting down across from me, "is that - Remember I told you Shao-lin comes from the Middle East?"

"Yes, *sensei*," I said.

"And you asked me if it came from the Babylonians?"

I nodded my head.

"How well do you know your own history?"

"Fairly well," I said.

"Then what if I said that Shao-lin comes from Babylonia but not from the Babylonians?"

I was stumped.

"Haven't you ever wondered," he went on, "how Elijah managed to kill two hundred priests of Baal on Mount Carmel?"

Suddenly I understood what he was getting at. "But that's impossible," I blurted.

"Shao-lin," he said, staring at me intently, "was the warrior art of the ancient Israelites."

"That's hard to believe," I said.

"Why? Because you've never heard of it? I tell you, it was a secret art, known only to the priestly class, the nobility. It wasn't taught to the ordinary people."

"But it's never mentioned, not even in the Bible."

"Exactly," he said. "When the Babylonians conquered, the nobility was led into exile. The ancient wisdom was divided and half of it was lost. By the time a few returned to Jerusalem, the physical side had been forgotten."

"But how do you know this? I mean, how do you know Shao-lin was Jewish?"

"Have you ever heard of the ten lost tribes?"

"Of course," I said.

"Well, they weren't lost. They fled. At least some of them did. Some of them went east to China and taught the Buddhist monks at Shao-lin. Others went west. They forgot everything, even their language. But they named places after themselves to mark their way. When the tribe of Dan crossed a difficult river, they called it the Danube and that's why my people are called Danish to this day."

"But that's ridiculous!" I said. "There's not a shred of evidence for what you say."

I regretted the words as soon as I had said them. His face set and then he stood up, slamming the table into my chest. I was pinned against the wall.

"Evidence!" he said, waving his fist under my nose. "This is my evidence! I could kill you with one blow. Where do you think I learned to do that, hey?"

He jammed the table even harder into my ribs.

"I don't know," I wheezed.

"Do you think I'm making this all up?"

"*Sensei*, I can't breathe..."

"I've humoured you long enough. I've told you the secret of Shao-lin. Now, obey!"

"What do you want me to do?"

"Stop arguing with me!"

"I'm sorry, *sensei*."

He tugged at his beard furiously. Then he exhaled and pulled the table away. I fingered my ribs.

"The physical must be reunited with the spiritual," he said. "We are living in a glorious age. East is meeting west. We are coming full cycle. The Dane is remembering that he is a Jew and you Jews must stop being so provincial. You are not the only chosen people. That is why you, half-Scottish and half-Jew, are going to be my first disciple. You are going to be a symbol to all the rest."

His eyes were shining and he went on haranguing me for the better part of an hour. I kept saying I was honoured and that I would do my best. Before he let me go, he said, "Remember, I know where you work. I know where you live. Don't disappoint me. If you do, I swear I will kill you."

"I'll be in class tomorrow," I said.

———

Outside, I walked slowly for half a block and then I ran as fast as I could all the way home. I packed my belongings and spent the rest of the night in the train station. The next morning, promptly at nine o'clock, I presented myself at the Jewish Agency. The secretary, a lovely girl with green eyes, black hair and a surgically improved nose, looked up at me and said, "Yes?"

"I want to volunteer for the Israeli army."

She handed me a form. Ten minutes later, a counsellor called me into his office.

"So you want to go to Israel," he said.

"I want to join the army."

"Nasser has kicked out the U.N. The port of Eilat is blockaded. Aren't you afraid there is going to be a war?"

"I think it's inevitable," I said.

"So, you heard we were recruiting?"

"No. It's my own idea."

"Tell me," he said. "Why, under 'mother's maiden name' do you write Sutherland?"

"Because that was her name. She converted."

"Not that it matters," he added quickly. He looked at my physique. "Frankly, we would pay your way anyway, under the Law of Return."

"The Law of Return," I said. "That entitles Jews anywhere in the world to go back to Israel, doesn't it?"

"That's what it says," he beamed.

"And the Jewish Agency pays?"

"That's right."

"But how do you know? I mean, how do you know that the person you're paying for is actually Jewish?"

He leaned across his desk. "Confidentially," he said, "in this day and age, if you're crazy enough to say you're Jewish, who's going to argue?"

"And that's it? That's the definition?"

"That's it."

———————

I got six weeks of training before the war broke out and they sent me to the front. I killed three Egyptians that I know of. One was a soldier who threw his gun away just as I squeezed the trigger.

As for my yarmulka, it made my head itchy under the thickened skull of my helmet. I took it off and lost it somewhere in the desert sand.

THE DEATH OF THE
WANDERING JEW

The white walls of Uzi's room were lined with snakeskins - fifty dark, wide, hanging hides, heads nailed to a slat of wood which ran a foot below the ceiling, some stretching almost to the floor, some gliding down behind the bed, the clothes bureau, the simple desk and chair, the few other utilitarian things which made up Uzi's spartan world. Sometimes, in the evening, after the day's work in the orchard, after the tasteless communal kibbutz meal, we would sit on the red tiled floor of his room and he would make two thimbleful cups of thick delicious Greek coffee and we would talk - more about him than about me.

He had been orphaned as a small child, he told me. His parents had been killed in a concentration camp - he had no memory of them, not even a photograph. The kibbutz had adopted him, raised him, had given him his totemic machine-gun name. It was his destiny, he believed, to live up to it, to be as hard, as merciless, as efficient - though this was not something he told me in so many words; was, rather, something I inferred from the set of his mouth, the calm, green, unhurried, uncomplicated movement of his eyes, so different from the nervous inquisitive insecurity I had known in the eyes of Jews in North America and which I had discovered in my own. Which was why, in my early twenties, hoping not so much to find my roots as to escape my past, I had come to Israel. I was attracted by its aura of manliness, its pioneer spirit, its military prowess, a prowess I had seen during the war of '67.

So I was attracted to Uzi. I admired him from the moment I saw him striding through a lane of apple trees towards the sorting machine at the edge of the orchard where I worked. He was not tall but he carried himself like a Samson, erect, his hair blond and matted, his head set on a powerful neck which rose from broad muscular shoulders. He was wearing a faded pair of shorts but no shirt and no boots and I was struck, when he came closer, by the mud-caked callouses I could see on the sides of his feet. I was surprised because I had been warned about a deadly kind of viper that lived among the apple trees - its venom, I was told, able to kill a man in less than a minute - and so, as soon as I decently could without making myself look like an awestruck sissy, I casually asked in my best Hebrew, "Isn't that dangerous?"

Uzi's head swivelled in my direction and his green level gaze took me in. His eyes travelled down my arm to where my finger was pointing at his naked feet. He looked back at me, steadily, guilelessly.

"I am not afraid of snakes," he said quietly, in what would have been remarkably good English except that the way he clipped his words gave him an accent which sounded, ironically, faintly German. "Tonight, after eating, you will come to my room. I will show you something."

———

What he showed me was the fifty snakeskins. He had caught them himself - with his bare hands.

"With your bare hands!" I exclaimed, my eyes popping. But Uzi mis-read my expression and thought I did not believe him.

"No, truly," he said. "I turn over stones in the field. Often a snake is there. If snake is there, I whirl my hands like this." Sitting cross-legged in front of me on the tile floor, Uzi held out his arms and turned his hands rapidly from side to side.

"Always the snake stands up, moves back and forth between my hands, trying to make up his mind - which hand to strike? But the snake can see only one hand at a time. Snake must focus before he can strike, must stop moving. That is the chance - maybe less than a second - next second the snake is going to strike. I use the hand snake can not see. Very, very fast, I grab him here."

Uzi's hand shot out towards my neck. A trained reflex, I instinctively used a Shao-Lin Karate technique to block the blow and caught him by the wrist. He was surprised, impressed. A slow, mischievous grin spread across his face - and marked the beginning of our friendship.

After that we wrestled often on the grass outside his hut. He told me about the American girlfriend who had taught him English - by

94

playing Bob Dylan songs and explaining the meaning of the lyrics - and often we listened to the records she had left. I told him how I wanted to be a writer and how, and why, I had come to Israel. We took turns speaking Hebrew and English, correcting each other's mistakes - me saying, for instance, that in English a snake is an "it", not a "him". He told me he was a Commander in the Paratroops - an elite, hush-hush group designed to fight behind enemy lines. He described the training and the raids. And one day he walked barefooted up to me at the edge of the orchard and said: "This *Shabbat*, you will come with me?"

"Sure. Where're we going?"

"I will show you the back country. Maybe we catch a snake."

The sun was hot, the wild grasses burnt and dusty. We climbed through a slanting pine wood, my boots slipping on the floor of dry needles. When we paused to catch our breath, Uzi said every tree had been planted by Jewish settlers.

"Using money from America," I teased.

"And Europe, and Australia, and South Africa."

Which was true: The kibbutz Hebrew teacher had said my class of fifty fellow-students represented every continent on Earth except Antarctica - an ingathering of the Exiles.

We climbed steadily for another hour before I asked where we were going.

"You'll see," Uzi answered.

We wandered through the cinder-brick streets of a Druse village - invisible in a cleft in the hills until we came upon it - Uzi telling me that no outsider had ever been allowed to see their secret ceremonies; that if someone offered us a cup of coffee, we must refuse; if asked again, we could refuse or accept, the choice was up to us; but if asked a third time, we must accept. Not to accept, he told me, would be regarded as an insult to Arab hospitality and would poison relations between the village and the kibbutz.

At the back end of the village, the climb became steeper and we had to use our hands to grab onto rocks and roots and pull ourselves upwards. My shirt became soaked with sweat. I was about to ask, again, where we were going when suddenly we reached the crest and I found myself staring up at a gleaming white statue of a fierce bearded man holding a sword high in the air above me.

"This is Mount Carmel," Uzi said. "And that is the prophet Elijah. At one point, it was a very low point, he was the only Jewish prophet left in the whole country. Here he killed the priests of Baal and then he ran, faster than the chariot of the king, all the way to the Valley of Jezreel."

Uzi planted his bare feet wide and pointed majestically at the valley we could see shimmering in a blue haze twenty miles away. We stood there a long time, staring in silence at the brown, wrinkled face of the land far below.

"That is my mother and my father," Uzi said. I looked at him and saw that his eyes were filmed with tears and so I looked away. "Come," he said after a while, touching my shoulder lightly. "There is someone I want you to meet."

He was naked except for a fraying grey loincloth. He was very thin and very old. His chest and stomach were a cross-hatch of glistening lines and creases. His beard was a tangled mix of white and black. His hair was pulled tight against his scalp and held in place by an elastic band. His greeting smile showed a gap of smooth pink gum between two large ivoried teeth. When he spoke his tongue clapped the palate of his mouth and made his Hebrew soft and sibilant like the sound of water flowing over stones. He was a hermit and lived in a cave in the foothills of Mount Carmel. Uzi told me that the old man believed himself to be the Wandering Jew.

"After the war, when I was a boy all alone, he looked after me in the refugee camp. We came to Israel on the same boat."

Uzi had survived the war in a Christian orphanage. Somehow, the old man had survived Auschwitz. Now we were seated on the ground in the shade of the canvas awning which, in bad weather, served as the flap on the entrance to his cave. The old man caught me peeking at the blue tattoo on his emaciated arm and, laughing soundlessly, held it out for closer inspection.

"When we got off the train," he said, me straining to understand him, Uzi supplying the meaning of words he knew I had missed, "even many people younger than me had already died. The Germans selected the strong young men and the pretty girls; women and children and old people like me they sent to the showers." Again he laughed soundlessly. His long, worn fingers curled around his knees and he drew himself forward and peered at me. "Uzi tells me you are a writer," he went on unexpectedly. I said that that was what I was hoping to be. The old man glanced at the ground demurely, shrugged his bony shoulders. I realized that I had been unable to distinguish his pupils in the tenebrous black of his imperious, heavy-lidded eyes.

"It does not matter if you do not believe me," he said. "Perhaps what I tell you will make you a good story."

"There is always truth in a good story," I replied diplomatically.

But the old man had closed his eyes and was no longer listening. Instead his lips began moving and it seemed to me that his two ivory incisors and Uzi and I were stones over which flowed the river of his words. "I have been burned many times - in Spain, in Albania, in Poland, in Germany many times. In Rome they made me run naked around the ghetto walls and then they boiled me in the fat of a pig. But I never died. Always I was born again - a little boy running and jumping and playing in the sunshine and then, suddenly, one day, I would remember who I was. I would remember all my past lives and everything that had happened to me."

The old man opened his eyes. His thin arm swept the thistled gullies and hills of the surrounding countryside. "I was born here. All my family - my mother and father, my wife, my children - they are all buried here."

He paused, shrugged a shrug of resignation, smiled his astonishing fang-toothed smile. "My needs are simple. God provides. He sends rain twice a year. I have fruit."

He pointed to two small trees - an apple and a fig - growing incongruously out of the stony ground a stone's throw away.

"Are you hungry, boys? Would you like to pick a fruit?"

Seeing how little he had, I answered politely, "No, thank you."

"Please, accept my hospitality. The fig is very good, very sweet. It is refreshing."

I glanced at Uzi who nodded back at me.

"The second time is our choice, right?"

"Yes," Uzi said . "But he will ask again." We both got to our feet. The fig we came back with was green and small and wrinkled but Uzi told me it was ripe. He showed me how to split it with my thumbnail. Inside, the flesh was pink and labial. I laughed and, biting into my half, I said I wondered whether this had been the fruit of the Tree of Knowledge or the fruit of the Tree of Life.

However, the old man had closed his eyes and was telling his story again: "I studied the Talmud, the Cabbala. I studied science, history, philosophy. I amassed great wealth. I had many wives, many children. Each time I smelled the smoke of my own burning body, I cried, 'O Lord, King of the Universe, I have seen enough. Release me from this witness.' Each time I was born again and then, suddenly, one day all the memories would come back and there a little boy would be, standing in the sunshine, appalled by his memories. Ecclesiastes, *Koheleth*, was wrong: it is not death which makes life a vanity. Death is the gift of a loving God. I look forward to it with rejoicing and it will come soon now, I know."

The old man fell silent. I thought perhaps he was dozing in the afternoon sun. Meanwhile, my logical, sceptical mind was busily at work finding a flaw in what he had told me. "There's one thing I do not understand," I said. "If each time you die you are reborn, how can you be so old now? Did you not die at Auschwitz?"

The old man's eyes flew wide open. "But that is the point I am making! When I survived the gas, they threw me into the crematorium anyway. Of course, I expected to be burned alive. I expected the same torture I had suffered before. Instead, I found myself in the fiery furnace and I did not burn. My body was in the flames and I felt nothing. When they opened the doors, I walked out."

"But what about the men who saw this happen?" I protested. "Surely they would have told the world about such a miraculous thing."

Again, the old man shrugged and glanced demurely at the ground in front of him. "They would have," he agreed, "if a Jew had not killed them."

"You mean, you killed them?"

The old man flicked his tongue between his teeth and ignored the question. "For a long time I wondered what was the meaning of what had happened. Only lately have I understood. I did not die in the Holocaust because the Jewish people died; I have not been reborn because the Jewish people have been reborn."

He sighed, stared at his arid domain with inward-seeing eyes. "It was Passover. I was on a pilgrimage to Jerusalem. There was a crowd in the street - a young rabbi dragging a cross. He asked me for a drink of water. I was too terrified. There were Roman soldiers everywhere. I have been wandering the world, waiting for the Messiah to deliver me, ever since."

The eyes focused, burned into me, then turned slowly away and fixed on Uzi. "If, now, the Wandering Jew has returned to Israel; if, now, the Wandering Jew is dying, then the Messiah must have come.I, who survived the Holocaust, I tell you, the Messiah has been born."

———

On the way back to the kibbutz Uzi and I overturned a large boulder at the edge of a dry ravine. Under it was a long, thick, blue-black snake. The snake reared and poised to strike one of Uzi's whirling hands. Uzi grabbed it behind the neck and killed it instantly.